Williams

A Joyous
Heart

"We Welcome Your Response"
CHOICE BOOKS

407 E Mt. Vernon
Metamora, IL 61548

Carrie Bender

A Joyous Heart

HERALD PRESS
Scottdale, Pennsylvania
Waterloo, Ontario

Library of Congress Cataloging-in-Publication Data
Bender, Carrie
    A joyous heart / Carrie Bender.
    p. cm. — (Miriam's journal ; 3)
    Sequel to: A winding path.
    ISBN 0-8361-3668-3
    1. Farm life—Pennsylvania—Fiction. 2. Family—Pennsylvania—
Fiction. 3. Amish—Pennsylvania—Fiction. 4. Women—Pennsylva-
nia—Fiction. I. Title. II. Bender, Carrie, Miriam's journal ; 3.
PS3552.E53845J6 1994
813'.54—dc20
                                                              94-5836
                                                              CIP

The paper used in this publication is recycled and meets the minimum
requirements of American National Standard for Information
Sciences—Permanence of Paper for Printed Library Materials, ANSI
Z39.48-1984.

Scripture quotations and allusions imbedded in the text are based on
the *King James Version of the Holy Bible*, with some adaptation to
current English usage. For a list of references, see the back of the book.

A JOYOUS HEART
Copyright © 1994 by Herald Press, Scottdale, Pa. 15683
    Published simultaneously in Canada by Herald Press,
    Waterloo, Ont. N2L 6H7. All rights reserved
Library of Congress Catalog Number: 94-5836
International Standard Book Number: 0-8361-3668-3
Printed in the United States of America
Book design by Paula M. Johnson
Cover art and illustrations by Joy Dunn Keenan
Series logo by Merrill R. Miller

03 02 01 00 99 98 97 96 95 10 9 8 7 6 5 4 3
20,000 copies in print

*To all who have gone through
the valley of the shadow of a child's death
and emerged with a joyous heart*

♥

Contents

♥

The Author

The author's pen name is Carrie Bender. She is a member of an old order group. With her husband and children, she lives among the Amish in Lancaster County, Pennsylvania.

Counting Blessings

*F*inally, I found the time for journal-writing again. We were late in getting the fall work done. Then there was a flurry of weddings and all-day quiltings, the butchering, not to mention the daily chores, carrying in coal, and carrying out ashes for the kitchen range and the parlor stove.

Now, I guess I can say I'm caught up, and I sent my *Maud* (maid), Barbianne, home for a few weeks before spring housecleaning begins. I'd like to do some reading and writing, maybe hook a rug or two, and spend leisure time with the children, reading to them and playing with them. Right now all five of them are taking a nap, and I am alone in the kitchen.

It's cozy in here, the teakettle is humming a tune on the range, and the clock on the mantle ticks gaily away. Outside, big flakes of snow are gently floating down, putting a clean white coat on top of snow already on the ground.

Through the window I can see the bird feeder Nate put up for me, to help our feathered friends that make themselves at home in our backyard along the creek this winter. A pair of pert little chickadees (my favorite) are at the feeder now, darting in and out until a saucy jay chases them away.

A bright red cardinal flew regally in, followed by his

mate. Then a tufted titmouse grabbed a sunflower seed and retreated to a perch in the old oak tree to dine on it. Nuthatches, woodpeckers, and finches also frequent the feeder regularly. Watching them all is a lovely pastime for all of us.

By my side I have a stack of colorful seed magazines, filled with pictures of delicious-looking vegetables and picture-perfect flower gardens. Now is the time to dream about my weedfree garden. Dreaming about it is almost as much fun as achieving it.

Although tomorrow is Valentine's Day and not Thanksgiving Day, I've been sitting here feeling thankful and counting my blessings. I have Nate, my good, kindhearted husband, and five precious children. Dora (our foster daughter) will be five years old in April, and the rest all have birthdays in March. The twins, Peter and Amanda, will be three, Sadie will be two, and in a few weeks little Crist will be one.

Dora is the beauty of the family, Peter is the sturdy little farmer boy, sweet little Amanda has health problems with glutaric aciduria but is doing well at the present. Sadie is our cute, placid sunshine girl, and little Crist already shows signs of being the mischief of the family.

Then there are friends and relatives, such as Isaac and Rosemary and their family in faraway Minnesota, who just announced the arrival of little Isaac, Jr. Father Isaac is preaching the Word there, and Rosemary is a wonderful helpmate for him. Allen and Polly and their children are dear to my heart, too, and a letter from them makes glad my day.

Dearly beloved Priscilla and Henry are happily married and living nearby. Henry is adjusting well to our Amish living and fits right in with the rest of the men at Sunday church services. Priscilla is the picture of health, and we're all hoping it will stay that way, with her blood disorder a thing of the past. She has resigned herself to letting us raise Dora as our daughter, satisfied with having Dora one day a week.

Grandpa Daves are high on the list of our blessings, since they volunteered to be foster grandparents to our children. We love them, warts and all, as well as if they were blood relatives.

Then there is Rudy, our *Gnecht* (hired man), and Barbianne, our *Maud* (maid). They're always together, at least every chance they get, it seems. It's a case of "O whistle, and I'll come to you, my lad" (Burns), for Barbianne likes nothing better than to be outside working with Rudy, and I believe he enjoys her company. They are both good, de-

pendable helpers, and the children love them greatly and look up to them.

What I am most thankful for these days is that Nate has gone to file income tax returns. He confessed (turned himself in, rather) that he hadn't been paying, and now he has paid every last cent of his obligation, including late-payment fines. There will be no trial or hearing, as I had feared, no jail sentence (I fervently thank the Lord), and we won't lose this farm and our home by the creek.

As for the Foster farm, we're not sure yet about that—maybe if we save and scrimp (beyond being thrifty), do without some things we'd like to have, and work hard, we'll be able to keep it. Time will tell. It doesn't matter that much to me, but I can tell that Nate has his heart set on holding onto it if he can.

He even said we'll live on fried mush and dried beans, if necessary, and work twenty-four hours a day plus half the night, if that's what it takes. I'm sure he was just joking, though.

It's so nice to see him feeling chipper and good-natured again, now that his "burden of sin" has rolled off his back, and he has made things right. There's no sense in us weak mortals carrying the heavy load of our sins, when Jesus has already borne them and will freely forgive. The Lord will remove them from us as far as the east is from the west, if we but confess and repent. I've been feeling joyous and lighthearted ever since.

It's time to take my whole-wheat bread out of the oven, judging by the wonderful aroma in the kitchen, and I hear the pitter-patter of little feet coming down the stairs. My sweet, pink-cheeked, tousle-headed dears are waking up, and I'm glad to see them. I think we'll make some red valentine hearts together, with lace out around and a verse in the middle, to send to Matthew, Rosabeth, and Mary. Valentine's Day is for celebrating love! "My heart rejoices in the Lord. . . . I rejoice in your salvation." ❧

March 2

Oh my soul, why art thou vexed?
Let things go even as they will;
Though to thee they seem perplexed,
Yet His order they fulfill.
—A. H. Francke

I'm worn to a frazzle tonight, and my nerves feel frayed at the edges. We received word today that Nate's cousin, an elderly man from Ohio, has passed away, and Nate got a sudden notion to travel along with a vanload to attend the funeral. I've been busy, scurrying around and getting his clothes ready, and packing his suitcase. Little Crist was unruly and mischievous, Dora and Peter fought over a toy, and Sadie wasn't feeling well and followed me around, begging to be held.

Finally Nate was ready (the van driver only had to wait ten minutes). With a wave of the hand, he was off. Peter ran after him, crying and screaming, because he wanted to go along, too, and I paddled him. Dora didn't act like that, but she sat in a corner pouting for half an hour, because she couldn't go, and I didn't know whether or not I should paddle her.

Rudy came in and wondered why everyone was so glum and unhappy. Finally I got a half-decent meal on the table, and after we'd eaten, we all went out to help with the chores. By that time my head was aching fiercely. I forgot to turn off a faucet and flooded a calf pen, which made an extra half hour's work for me.

The children seemed unusually boisterous, and I realized (though I am loathe to admit it) that Nate can do more with them than I can. Even Rudy's word is not law like Nate's is. At last the day was over and everyone in bed. I crawled into bed, but not to sleep. The house creaked eerily, and something thumped upstairs. I sat up, my heart beating wildly.

The March wind shrieked around the corners of the house, and the wheel of the windmill whined and clanked as the wind swung to the south. I usually love that sound, but when Nate's not here, everything is different. Cocky began to bark outside the front door, and I fearfully went to the window, expecting to see a burglar somewhere.

A few thick clouds scudded in front of the moon, and the branches tossing in the wind cast eerie shadows on the lawn. What if the "thieves" decided to strike again, while Nate is gone? I shivered and got back into bed.

Please Lord, don't let the thieves come tonight.

To divert myself, I reached for my journal and pen and began writing. My heart aches tonight, for the young widows with growing families to raise, without a husband's help. For them, there is no thinking that "in a few days daddy will be home, and everything will be all right again."

Oh, God, help them and strengthen them, and give them the courage they need to go on. 🐝

Somehow we survived the few days that Nate was gone. Last evening I was puttering around the kitchen rather late, doing some baking after the children and Rudy were in bed, when someone knocked insistently on the washhouse door. My first impulse was to flee up the stairs and wake Rudy, and I started for the stair door, heart beating wildly.

Yet something made me turn around and unlock the door, and there stood Nate, suitcase in hand, smiling broadly! I welcomed him joyously. Actually, I thought he never looked quite so good to me before. I hadn't been expecting him until today, so it was a happy surprise.

"I'm as hungry as a bear," Nate declared, sniffing the air. "What smells so good? I haven't had any lunch nor supper. The van broke down just outside town, and I walked the rest of the way home."

So I quickly heated some soup, made a few sandwiches for him, and took the shoofly pies out of the oven. After Nate had eaten, we sat and talked until midnight. The March winds howling outside suddenly were friendly again, the house-creaking sounds were dear and familiar instead of frightening, and the clanging of the windmill was a dear lovely sound again.

Nate stretched and quoted a favorite line, "Be it ever so humble, there's no place like home" (Payne). He kicked off his shoes and stuck his feet into the bake oven of the range to warm them. Cocky barked outside the door, and I thought, Let the thieves come and steal. What does it matter? Nate's home! ❧

March 12

*R*obins are hopping around, cocking their heads, and listening for earthworms. The wind is still brisk, but if the robins come back, "can spring be far behind?" (Shelley).

This morning Priscilla drove over to take Dora along for the day and to pick up her garden seeds. I couldn't help but notice that she seemed happy and excited about something as she hopped off the buggy and tied her horse. Her cheeks were pink and flushed, and her eyes sparkled.

"You are radiant," I told her. "What's up? Is anything new?"

"Yes, oh yes!" she replied. "If I look half as radiant as I feel, it surely must be noticeable. Henry's coming over with me tonight when we bring Dora back, and then we'll tell you." She gave me a knowing look and a secretive smile as she drove off with Dora.

Sooo! If it's what I think it is, then Henry's still got some of his *englisch* (non-Amish) ways. Coming over together to

18

break news like that, probably right in front of the children yet! Oh well, maybe they won't catch the meaning of it. Priscilla probably told Dora all about it already. I must admit, though, that I'm almost as eager as they are. After all, they've already been married for eight and a half months.

Every so often I tell Dora again that Priscilla is her real mother, that her real daddy died, and that now Nate and I are her mother and dad. Henry thought it would be better for her to stay here because she's been here since she was a little baby.

I didn't want to wait so long to tell her that it would come as a shock to her. She seems to accept the situation well and doesn't seem bothered about it. Almost every day I marvel at her beauty and her fine, sensitive features. Her thoughts seem to flit across her face, and you can almost tell what she's thinking by her expression and her features.

Yesterday afternoon she came and threw her arms around me. "I love you, Mam."

I hugged her back. "I love you, too."

She still hung around me, and I thought she seemed guilty about something.

"Is anything wrong?" I asked her gently.

She shook her head, then burst into tears, rubbing her eyes with her fists.

"Dora!" I exclaimed, feeling real alarm by now. "Tell me what's wrong!"

"Come." She beckoned with her hand, so I followed her up the stairs and into the spare room. There on the floor, smashed into many pieces, lay the washbowl and pitcher set Allen had given me when I worked for him and he was a widower. In her play, she had knocked it off the nightstand.

I laughed out loud. "Don't feel bad about it, Dora. If that's all that's wrong, cheer up. Everyone accidentally breaks things sometimes."

She smiled through her tears and was happy again. Actually, the pitcher set had no sentimental value for me at all. Now, if Nate had given it to me, it would've been another story! ❧

March 20

*M*y Father, what am I that all
Thy mercies sweet, like sunlight fall
    So constant o'er my way?
That Thy great love should shelter me,
And guide my steps so tenderly
    Through every changing day?
                    —*Unknown*

Spring is such a lovely time of year, and garden-planting is one of my favorite tasks. I guess I should've waited until next week when Barbianne comes back, but the ground was fit, the air was balmy and warm, and the robins sweetly singing. Somehow it all got into my blood, and I just had to go out and dig into the moist, dark earth.

I thought the children could play nicely in the sandbox while I sowed the seeds, but they had other ideas. They all wanted to help and had me thoroughly confused as to what goes where. Oh, well, if the carrots come up in the row of peas, and the radishes with the red beets, at least I'll know who to blame it on. They're never too young for us to instill in them a love of gardening. ❧

*O*ur first day of real warm, summerlike weather. The leaves popped out on the maple trees today. That miracle never ceases to amaze me. One day they're still tightly curled up in their buds, and the next, lo and behold, real green leaves are open and growing!

Even Peter noticed the difference. "Mam, look! The leaves are out! Did Jesus make those leaves while I was taking my nap?"

I explained to him that God made the sun shine bright, the warm sunshine opened the leaf buds, and the sap inside the trees caused them to grow. He sat there, a puzzled look on his ruddy face, trying to figure that out.

The sun shining through the window made Peter's hair shine reddish, and I thought for the hundredth time that he looks more like Nate every day. He's usually not satisfied with a simple explanation but has to figure things out thoroughly from every angle, asking dozens of questions. Some, surprisingly intelligent for his age, even have me floundering for an appropriate answer.

Peter is sturdy and rotund, and no one would ever guess by their appearance that he and Amanda are twins. She is dark haired and frail-looking, and has an almost angelic expression on her face. Maybe that's why Nate sometimes calls her Little Angel. She is so quiet and causes me so little trouble that I'm afraid she sometimes gets pushed into the background by her active and demanding siblings.

Oh, God, help me to be a good mother to each child, giving each one what they need, and each their share of attention. Help me to accept each child without conditions and learn to enjoy them for the special persons they are.

The supreme happiness of life for them is knowing that they are loved. Do my children know they are loved? As parents, the way we extend love to our children deeply affects their ability to relate effectively to others.

Lord, help us to be a beacon of your love. ❧

May 29

Strawberries and peas are in full swing, and I'm so glad for Barbianne's help. Rudy helps with the picking, too, between haymaking and planting. Of course, they're always working side by side.

Today while I was busy capping berries at the kitchen table, Rudy came in with two big bowls of strawberries. No matter how busy he is, he always has time for a few kind words for Amanda, or a pat on her head, or swinging her up in the air, which makes her shriek with laughter. He has a soft spot in his heart for her, and he calls her "My Mandy Girl."

Whenever he says that, Barbianne wrinkles up her nose at him. It's obvious that she wants to be his girl, and Rudy doesn't seem to resent it. He laughs and winks charmingly at her. There's definitely something special brewing between them.

This time Barbianne was still out in the patch, and Rudy put Amanda down and came over to me. Half jokingly he asked me, "Say, Miriam, you know Barbianne as well as anyone, so please tell me exactly what you think of her. Do you think she'll make me a good wife?" He laughed as he spoke, pretending it was all only a funny joke. But underneath it all, I could tell he was in earnest.

I smiled. "I thought you seemed more than a little interested in her."

"I am," he admitted. "About ninety-five percent of the time, I think I'd like to start dating her. But sometimes I have my doubts."

"I think she'd make a fine wife for you. I like her friendly, open personality, and I think she's more mature than she was when she came to work for us."

"Did you notice it, too?" he asked eagerly. "I thought she'd changed a lot, but I wasn't sure if it was just wishful thinking on my part."

"No, especially since she's in the class taking instruction for baptism, I noticed a difference," I assured him. "She's more steady and serious minded, more thoughtful of other's feelings. She's good with the children, too, and that's high on my list of priorities for a maid."

Rudy went out the door whistling a glad tune. &

June 16

*R*oses and honeysuckle time once again, and I'm also a year older. Nate isn't one for remembering birthdays, but somehow, that doesn't bother me a bit. He came in today for a drink and enthusiastically told me that "the thieves in the trailer," as we call them, are apparently moving out. A moving van is parked there, and they're carrying out furniture and belongings.

That's good news! We've had so much trouble with them, though lately we haven't seen or heard much of them. We'll probably never know why they singled us out for harassment, or what their motive was. I have to think of the words in Proverbs, "He that despises his neighbor sins." I know we should love them and pray for them, but with their deeds, it is hard to do.

I think I'll step outside and take a few deep breaths of that newly mown clover hay. Barbianne would say the scent is heavenly. ☙

July 16

*C*ompany's coming for dinner tomorrow! Grandpa Daves and Henry and Priscilla are bringing surprise visitors. I don't know who they might be, but I have an idea—possibly Gloria Graham and her new husband, and Kitty Kat, or the Rogers. I hope they're the ones because it's been quite awhile since I've seen Stacey, their Down's syndrome child.

Just when I let Barbianne go home for a three-day weekend, I got news of the visit. Now I have to get ready alone. I've been scrubbing the house, mowing the lawn, trimming the grass along the walks, tending flowerbeds, baking, and making desserts—or rather, trying to do all of these.

Little Crist is into everything these days. He scoots up on chairs, tilts them, and takes a tumble. You'd think he would learn not to do it again, but as soon as his tears are dried, he climbs right up again. I have to keep the chairs lying on their sides, and I have a yardstick through my sewing machine drawer handles so he can't pull them open.

Once he grabbed my big sharp scissors and ran off with

them, surprisingly fast for a sixteen-month old. I held my breath until I had safely taken them from him. He's small for his age, but wiry and quick.

None of the others were as active as he is, and Sadie is quite the opposite. Compared to him, she was and still is as good as gold. But, Elfin Crist, as I still call him sometimes, is lovable and charming in his own way, even with mischief dancing in his eyes and a roguish smile on his lips. Whatever will become of him? ❦

July 19

Giving thanks unto the Father who has made us fit to be partakers of the inheritance of the saints in light."

I could hardly believe my eyes when the two carriages drove in before lunchtime. Who was that man sitting on the front seat beside Henry? No, it couldn't be true! I pinched myself to see if it was for real. Isaac, and Rosemary, holding baby Isaac, Jr., in the backseat beside Priscilla! In the other carriage were Grandpa Daves, with Matthew, Rosabeth, and Anna Ruth.

So happy was I that I felt like dancing a jig, which would be an undignified way for an old lady to act. Matthew ran in first, and when he saw me, he suddenly turned shy. I couldn't believe how tall he had grown and that he's actually almost seven years old. My, how time flies!

There were lots of tears and laughter, hugging and embracing among us women, and hearty handshakes among the men. Henry had boarded at Isaac's place for awhile, so he was almost family to them, too.

We spent the afternoon talking and reminiscing, satisfying the deep longing in our hearts for a time of sweet fellowship together. We all felt hallowed and enriched by it. They are planning to attend church in our district tomorrow, and Isaac will bring the message. For quite awhile already, I've had a longing to hear him preach once again. It seems too good to be true.

Rosemary told many interesting stories about life in Minnesota, some scary ones. While most of the natives welcomed the Amish warmly into the area, a few were hostile to them and tried to get them to leave. One evening just as they all sat down at the table to eat supper, a car drove past, and there was a loud explosion, the sound of a gun being fired.

They found a small bullet hole in the front hall door. It appeared that someone had deliberately shot into their house. Then last summer Isaac found a patch of strange-looking plants smack in the center of one of his huge cornfields. (They say the fields around here look like dolly patchwork quilts, compared to the size of the fields there.) He called for county officials to check the plants, and they turned out to be marijuana. They still haven't found out who put them there.

In the huge old tree in their yard, a pair of raccoons have a nest with four young ones. In the late evening hours, they hear them fighting and scrapping and sometimes screaming. A few times they've heard coyotes howling, a spine-tingling sound, according to Rosemary. I sure hope we can go to visit them sometime, for it sounds like quite an adventure.

Priscilla can no longer hide her condition, and neither would she try if she could. She is glowing with happiness and basks in the congratulations and comments from others. Henry freely talks about it. Sometimes I feel like asking Nate to have a chat with him, to tell him that's just not the way Amish do. But I hate to put a damper on his enthusiasm.

They all stayed for supper, too. After the chores were finished, we sat around the table and sang hymns until bedtime. They're starting for home already on Tuesday, and the rest of the time they'll spend with Rosemary's parents.

Thank you, heavenly Father, for enabling them to pay us this lovely visit. ❦

August 23

We've had ample rainfall this summer, and the cornfields are a sea of tall green stalks, each with a fat golden ear or two.

These days going to town is a hassle, so we don't go oftener than necessary. Streets and stores are full of tourists, flashing cameras and staring. Last time we went, Dora stamped her foot and said she's not wearing her bonnet.

I asked her, "Why ever not?"

Her answer was loaded with anger. "The last time I wore it to town, a boy pointed at it and said, 'Look at the girl's funny hat.' So I won't wear it again!"

Trying not to smile, Nate and I patiently explained to her why we wear bonnets. Soon she was her happy self again and cheerfully wore her bonnet.

This summer I'm teaching her to speak English because in a year's time she'll be starting first grade. Before she could understand English, we didn't have the problem of her catching what the tourists say.

On Saturday evening after the chores were finished, we loaded our supper and all the little ones into the boat and headed down the creek to a shady spot for a picnic. I try to have a family outing like this at least once a year, to create happy memories of family togetherness for the children.

It was a lovely evening, and the peacefulness and serenity of the woodland surroundings soothed our spirits. Once again it brought back memories of going boating with Nate that summer six years ago. A great blue heron majestically sailed off and perched on an old dead tree in the meadow. A fish splashed occasionally in the water.

I love to lie on my back and look up into the great green leafy boughs of the trees, with patches of blue shining through. Sadie came and nestled beside me, contented to watch the scenery. Meanwhile, Nate had his hands full trying to keep Crist from jumping headfirst into the water.

In the hazy August sky, the red sun began to set. Soon the night insects began to sing, and one by one the stars came out, twinkling in the dusky sky. Reluctantly we headed for home, guided by an occasional firefly flickering above the creek and in the trees, and by a sliver of moon rising above the treetops.

Sometimes I wish time would stand still so the children could remain with us as they are now, and so life could always be as peaceful and serene as it is now. ☙

September 17

*I*t is not that I feel less weak, but Thou
Wilt be my strength; it is not that I see

28

Less sin, but more of pardoning love with Thee,
And all sufficient grace. Enough! And now
All fluttering thought is stilled, I only rest
And feel that Thou art near,
And know that I am blest.
—*F. R. Havergal*

That is a blessed thought when all around are the thorns of choking care and responsibilities, robbing us of time to be spiritually attentive to God. Often the gentle and holy desires of the new nature are overpowered by the work and worry and hurry of the day.

On Thursday evening I had the playpen in the yard under the shade trees, as I often do in the evening while helping with the chores. In it I put Sadie and Crist, surrounded by their toys. Usually they keep each other entertained for about an hour, then usually Crist climbs out and joins us in the barn, and Sadie happily plays on by herself. The menfolk are extra busy this summer and fall, what with farming the Foster farm along with this one and starting silo-filling earlier.

When Crist joined me tonight, I was nearly finished with my chores. He was excited about something, chattering about a new puppy down by the creek, and tugging at my hand for me to go with him to see it.

I followed Crist outside the open barn door, just in time to see a full-grown red fox trotting up from the creek. He began to pick up speed and then with a mighty leap sailed over the playpen bars, attacking Sadie and biting her hand, then jumping out again. I still shudder to think about it.

I hollered for Nate, who was nearby, and he came running. As soon as he realized what had happened, he grabbed the gun he keeps in the toolshed beside the milk-house. Down by the creek, he shot the fox. There was no doubt about it, the fox was rabid!

We immediately went to the phone shanty and called a driver to take us to the clinic. Now she'll have to have those painful, expensive rabies shots. Poor little dear! The nurses sure made a fuss over her, how cute she is, such dark curly hair, round cheeks, big dark eyes, and such a sweet, trusting expression on her face, even through her tears.

Now we'll have to try to keep the children indoors until this rabies scare is over. Since there was one rabid animal around, there's bound to be more.

Oh, heavenly Father, please keep your protecting hand over them all. Let each one of them have a guardian angel, to protect them from danger, harm, and evil. ❧

October 31

*O*ctober's bright blue weather. The leaves along the creek were the most colorful ever, but according to Nate, I say that every year. Maybe so, but the splashes of reds, golds, and browns were a sight to behold. Several times Nate has talked of moving over onto the Foster farm. I didn't say much, but it sure would spite me to leave our home by the creek.

This is our Sunday between church services, so we took a drive on the spring wagon just to enjoy the scenery. The ride brought back memories of just over a year ago when Nate confessed he hadn't been paying income tax. Things turned out better than I feared they would, and it seems like a miracle to me.

We also like our horse better than ever, maybe because we found out what it's like to have to put up with an old balker. Rudy and Barbianne are now both baptized members of the church, and my heart rejoices for them. I wonder why they haven't started dating. I guess if they would, one of them would have to find another job. At least I hope that's the reason, for by this time, I the matchmaker am hoping to see them paired off soon.

Last week Gloria Graham was here with Kitty Kat. She lives in town with her new husband, George, and Kitty Kat is still her spoiled, pampered baby. George doesn't seem to appreciate it at all, the way she fusses over the cat and dotes on her, and I can't say that I blame him a bit.

Sadie is doing well. I'll be so glad when she's finished with the treatments. I hate hiring a driver so much, and I can't understand why some people do it even when it wouldn't be necessary, to go shopping and to sales and what not. Somehow, it doesn't seem right. Next, the real purpose of not having cars will be defeated if we so freely go to worldly places with the neighbors, such as to the beach, farm shows, or restaurants.

May we all strive to be a light to those around us, and a good example to the next generation. ❧

*G*ood news! Henry and Priscilla are the parents of a six-pound nine-ounce little girl named Miriam Joy! I can hardly believe they actually named her after me. Now I'll have to give her a *kavli* (diaper basket for church). Henry wanted a biblical name, and

Priscilla said she wanted to name her after the person who helped her more than anyone else. I was touched by this and didn't feel that I deserved it.

Dora keeps begging to go over there nearly all the time, so I guess I'll let them have her for a week or two. She's a good little mother's helper and can run errands for Priscilla. Henry's going to do most of the housework, and once a week she'll have a neighbor girl to do the laundry and the weekly cleaning.

Today Nate and I drove over to see the baby, and they sure are a set of proud parents! She's a lovely baby, a dark-haired beauty, and yet I can't really say that she looks like Dora. Priscilla had told me she had her heart set on a home delivery, but Henry was much opposed to it. I had my doubts about it, too, since Priscilla had that blood disorder.

Apparently the doctor consented to it, and Henry relented and let his wife win that time. A capable midwife came to help them at the right time. I'm so happy for them, for already when they were married only six months, Priscilla confided to me that they were thinking of seeing a fertility doctor soon. Thankfully, that wasn't necessary. ❧

December 7

O love that passeth knowledge, thee I need;
  Pour in the heavenly sunshine, fill my heart;
Scatter the cloud, the doubting and the dread,
  The joy unspeakable to me impart.
          —*H. Bonar*

Our "joy unspeakable" seems rather dim just now. We are very worried about Amanda. She hasn't been well lately, and we had her to see the specialist. He says her health problems have nothing to do with her glutaric aciduria condition, and he doesn't really know what to do for her. If she's not better soon, he wants her hospitalized. The thought fills me with dread.

This morning the scenery outside the window cheered us, though, after a snow during the night. But I remember that three years ago we also had such a winter wonderland scene early in the season. It's so much nicer along the creek than anywhere else.

If tourists would flock to the area to see something like this, I wouldn't blame them at all, but if they come to see the Amish, . . . that's something else. We are human beings, same as anyone else, just living a little differently.

Amanda has been running a low-grade fever these days, and she seems quite tired, too tired even to play sometimes. I sit and rock her and read to her a lot of the time. I can't resist her when she says, in that sweet little voice of hers, "Mam, please hold me and rock me and read to me."

Her favorite book is "Jesus Loves the Little Children," with a sketch of Jesus on the cover, gathering little children to himself. Yesterday she asked wistfully, "When can I see the real Jesus, not just his picture?"

When I didn't answer right away, she added, "Do you think he would hold me like he does the children in the picture, and make me feel better?"

I couldn't answer her, my voice was too unsteady and tears too near the surface. But Dora (playing with her doll nearby) overheard and responded, "Oh, yes, when we get to heaven, Jesus wipes away all our tears and makes us feel

_33_

better. No one is ever sick in heaven.".

"Oh, I'm so glad." Amanda breathed a sigh of relief. That angelic smile of hers . . . suddenly I could bear it no longer. I escaped to the bedroom and let the tears flow freely. ✌

December 14

*A*manda is no better, and we've been thinking about calling the specialist and having her admitted to the hospital. Again we've been getting a lot of advice from well-meaning friends. I value the counsel of other parents of children with glutaric aciduria, but that's not what's causing her trouble this time. If her levels would be off, or any other symptom of glutaric aciduria, we'd have her under the specialist's care at the hospital, without reservation.

Yesterday we had an interesting letter from plain people in another denomination. They have two children with a hereditary disease similar to glutaric aciduria and had wonderful results doctoring with someone in Toronto. He is not a specialist, and he doctors with herbs, vitamins, colonics, iridology, and improving the overall body condition of his patients.

The letter writers' daughter was also tired a lot of the time, lost her appetite, ran a fever, and complained of aches and pains. Upon the advice of friends of theirs, they made an appointment with this doctor and got a driver to take them. They had an eight-hour drive to his office, so they rented a room nearby and stayed two weeks.

The day after their first appointment, the child improved remarkably and thereafter responded amazingly well to the treatments. When the two weeks were up, she was in top shape physically and full of energy.

It sounds too good to be true! Nate and I have been wondering whether this doctor would be able to help Amanda. I've been cherishing a secret hope in my breast, ever since I read the letter, that we could take Amanda to this doctor (if it's God's will) and that she, too, would be helped so much. I'm trying not to get my hopes too high, but I can't help but feel eager. Nate doesn't say much, but I can tell he's interested, too. It's like a ray of sunshine, a beacon of light, as we grope in the darkness. 🌿

December 17

I can't believe that we're actually getting ready to go, that God is making it possible. Bill, our local taximan, has rented a small motor home for us to travel in. He'll drive us to Toronto, stay the two weeks, then bring us home again. I'm praying for good driving conditions, that the roads won't be icy or snowy.

Amanda is no better; actually, she's gone backward a little. But our hopes for her are high now, and her glutaric acid levels haven't gone up.

Rudy and Barianne will keep the home fires burning, stay with the rest of the children, and do the chores. We start off at one o'clock today, and I've done all the last-minute packing. I'm sorry for the sake of the other children that we'll be gone over Christmas. They're cooperating beautifully, though.

Awhile ago I saw Dora throw her arms around Amanda

and say, "I love you, and I'm so glad God is going to make you all better."

Last night when Peter knelt to say his bedtime prayer, he added, "Dear Jesus, please make Amanda feel good like an angel."

His childish prayer sent a stab of fear into my heart, almost like a foreboding, but I quickly brushed it aside. Crist seems more grown-up this past while, more like a toddler than a baby, and not as mischievous. With a pang, I realized that my baby is growing up fast. How can I bear to leave him, and all of them, for two weeks?

I hugged them all and kissed them a lingeringly goodbye. Sadie was clinging to me, and I brushed away a tear. Peter proudly declared that he's going to feed the horses and Cocky while we're away, and help Rudy with the cows. Dora asked if she might stay with Priscilla and Henry while we're gone and help care for Baby Miriam, and we gave our consent.

Bill arrived with the mini-motor home. This is an answer to prayer. It'll be so much nicer for Amanda to have a bed and lie down while we're driving.

Oh, God, please be with us, and grant us safe traveling and help for Amanda. ❧

December 18

*W*hen we in darkness walk,
 Nor feel the heavenly flame,
Then is the time to trust our God,
 And rest upon his name.

—*A. M. Toplady*

I'm soo-oo weary of traveling that I feel like crying, Amanda was restless, but finally she has fallen asleep. I'm tired of seeing cars and trucks and highways. I keep thinking, if I'd be back home with my trees and the birds, away from the wearisome traffic, I could rest, rest, rest.

Is God here in all this noise and confusion, where there is no peace and serenity? Can I find him here, where I can't see his handiwork, his creations and lovely nature scenes—only churning wheels, grime, and smog?

I think of the pioneer women rolling westward in covered wagons. They were traveling for weeks and months at a time, and they must often have been weary of it. But how different things were then!

They traveled through virgin forests, to the music of birdsong, through fresh country air. There was no noise of cars and trucks, and each evening they camped under the stars. If they grew weary of riding, they could walk awhile until they were glad to ride again.

I think the worst kind of weariness is the kind that comes from doing nothing.

Oh, God, help me to count my blessings and to be contented. 🐝

December 20

We had our first appointment with Dr. Keith today. He examined Amanda thoroughly, probing, pushing, squeezing, and even checking her feet. Often he consulted a little black box with wires attached to it. I wonder what that was for.

She has to take over forty pills every day! Poor girl. That

was almost more than I could take, but we've come this far now, and I guess we'll go through with it. If only it wouldn't be so expensive! I was shocked when he told us what we owe him just for this one visit. Then multiply that yet by twelve!

Oh well, if it helps her, we surely won't complain. The hope that it will heal her is what keeps us going.

The doctor seems confident that his treatments will cure her. "In two weeks we'll have her rosy cheeked and feeling peppy," he declared.

He's a man of few words, and I don't quite know what to think of him. Sometimes he even seems rather remote and distant (Nate thought so, too).

We found a place to park the motor home for the two weeks we'll be here, at a campground five miles from the doctor's office. It has a little propane heater to keep us warm. Now already I'm longing for home and the rest of the children. I guess I might as well admit that I'm utterly homesick. 🍂

December 25

*T*hank God for kind friends! Gloria Graham picked up Rudy, Barbianne, Dora, Peter, Sadie, and Crist, and took them to her house. We had planned to call there (collect) and talk to each one in turn. The familiar sound of their dear voices brought the tears to my eyes. Being so far away from loved ones on Christmas Day is hard, but talking to them long distance is next best to being there.

It sounds like everything is going well at home, which

makes it easier for us being here. Rudy reported that one of our best cows has twin heifer calves, both big and healthy!

Barbianne had an *elendich* (pitiful) story: she tried her hand at making mince pies, and they turned out wonderfully nice. After she set them on the back porch bench to cool, Cocky and the cats gobbled them up.

She said she was as mad as a hornet, but by this time she could laugh about it, and I laughed heartily, too. I told her that as long as nothing worse than that happens, we'll be happy.

Dora had great stories about Baby Miriam and helping Priscilla. Peter told us, laughing, that a cow kicked him into the gutter, and he got all *mischdich* (covered with manure), but he wasn't hurt in the least. Then in a concerned voice, he wondered, "Is Amanda getting better?"

None of the other children thought to ask that. Does he have a greater concern or feel closer to her because he is her twin? I just wish I could've told him, Yes, she is a lot better.

However, the truth is, she hasn't shown any improvement yet, and I am more worried than I care to admit to Nate. I keep telling myself, "Maybe it just takes more time."

Sadie and Crist both told us to come home *SCHNELL* (quickly) and to buy them some toys. They giggled a lot and seem to be all right.

The streets of Toronto are decorated for Christmas, and the stores have Christmas carols playing. Joy and peace is the theme, but I don't feel it in my heart. Where is that sweet assurance that I had, that we are in the center of God's will, that whatever happens, it will work together for good? God seems far away, and I feel uneasy.

I wish we had put Amanda into a hospital closer to home where the specialist who knows her condition could check on her. Nate seems discouraged, too.

The people around here act as if we're something out of a zoo. I guess some of them have never seen Amish people before. Talking with the loved ones at home cheered me momentarily, but now I'm feeling more homesick than ever. There's a lump in my throat that I just can't seem to swallow. 🥨

December 27

Amanda's condition has made a turn for the worse, and I'm feeling downright panicky. We had an appointment with Dr. Keith at 4:00 p.m., but when we came to the office, the door was locked and no one was around.

It was all so strange. We had called him before starting out from our home, and he had assured us it's all right to come, over the Christmas holidays, and that he wouldn't be taking a vacation.

Bill, our driver, was indignant. He says he's beginning to feel that this doctor is one big hoax and not to be trusted. I'm afraid there's another sleepless night ahead for us. 🥨

December 28

This morning at 9:00 o'clock, we again drove to Dr. Keith's office in hopes that he might be there, but again, the door was locked. Bill pounded angrily on the door until a window on the second floor was pushed open. A woman in a pink nightgown (possibly the landlady) leaned out and talked to us.

"I'm sorry," she told us, "but Dr. Keith has left, without telling anyone where he was going. I think he was practicing medicine without a license and is afraid the police are on his trail."

Words cannot express the feeling of desolation and despair we felt as we turned away to hide our tears. Bill began to rave and rant over the doctor, shaking his fist for added emphasis.

The woman shrugged her shoulders. "I'm sorry, but I can't help you. I'm afraid it's your own fault. You should've checked his credentials before you parted with your money. You plain people are much too gullible." She slammed the window down.

"The money!" I spat out. "What does money mean to us now? We've wasted a precious two weeks instead of getting real help for Amanda. Dr. Keith is nothing but a quack doctor!" The words had a bitter taste in my mouth.

"Well, we can't do anything more around here," Nate stated in disgust. "Let's start home immediately and get Amanda into a hospital as soon as possible."

My tears flowed freely as we prepared for the trip home. I felt crushed and betrayed. It wasn't fair. Hadn't we been seeking God's will? Did God mislead us, or did we misread him? The latter, of course.

My tears flowed with shame and humiliation, chagrin and despair. I had been so sure of myself, so hopeful, that I didn't wholeheartedly pray for God's guidance in the matter and wait for his leading. Now we were suffering for it, and Amanda most of all. ⚜

The trip home seemed like a nightmare. It began to snow, and the roads became treacherous and icy. Amanda's breathing was quick and shallow, and her face was flushed. In New York state, we decided to stay with an Amish family (almost complete strangers to us) for the night, in hope that the roads would be better the next morning.

During the night, Nate and I took turns sitting up with Amanda, in the warm kitchen where she lay on the sofa. Once when I walked past a mirror and happened to glance at my reflection, I was shocked to see deep, dark, racoon-like circles under my eyes.

Amanda was restless but had a smile for me when I took my turn sitting up with her after midnight. Toward morning I heard a snowplow chugging past and was glad. I hoped we could get an early start for home.

Lydia, the lady of the house, was soon up and bustling busily about, frying mush and eggs, and setting the table in the big country kitchen. I felt a surge of thankfulness for this family of like precious faith, who extended such gracious hospitality to us.

"I sure hope Amanda will be feeling a lot better soon," Lydia encouraged us, sympathetically. "Did you say you had her with a doctor in Toronto?"

"Yes, we did." I didn't want to talk about it.

"And he couldn't help her much? Hmmm, that's too bad. Did you ever consider getting someone to powwow for her?"

"What?" I looked sharply at Lydia.

"Powwowing. There's a lady up in the next county who

can powwow. They say she has the power to stop a dangerous flow of blood, and also pain and inflammation. She won't accept any pay for it, either."

I sat down in a chair, feeling shocked. I had heard old stories of Amish people who could powwow, but I didn't know whether or not one should believe them. After all, they were from nearly a century ago.

Just then Nate and Levi, the man of the house, came in from the barn for breakfast, and the children were coming downstairs, so the subject was changed. I decided then and there that powwowing was something I didn't know enough about to want to have anything to do with it. If it was God's will to heal Amanda, he could do it without that. If it wasn't his will, well—we weren't interested in a healing that wasn't from God.

Soon we were ready to leave, and after eight more hours of traveling torture, we pulled in at the hospital. We had stopped at a pay phone and called the specialist. He had made reservations for us at the hospital, and they were waiting for us.

The doctor gave us a why-didn't-you-bring-her-sooner look, but seeing our stricken faces, he wisely refrained from saying anything.

They took Amanda away for tests, and I was glad for a chance to be alone. I simply couldn't blink away any more tears nor continue clearing my throat to keep my voice steady. My body and spirit were on the verge of collapse.

Come, Lord, and show your mercy, for I am helpless, overwhelmed, and in deep distress. See my sorrows, feel my pain, and forgive my sins, for I am filled with remorse. If only. . . . ❦

 O ur homecoming was not the joyful affair we had planned it to be. Peter was the first to raise the question, "Where's Amanda?" There was a puzzled look on his face.

I sat down and gathered the children around me. How could I ever explain it to them while my own feelings were so remorseful, my emotions so raw?

When Rudy came in, he asked cheerfully, "Where's my Mandy girl?"

Barbianne gave him a look intended to silence him, and Peter ran over and explained, *"Dee Amanda is schlimm grank un in da hospital* (Amanda is badly sick and in the hospital)."

Sadie began to cry, hiding her face in my skirts, and I wanted to cry with her. Little Crist was napping, and Dora was at Priscilla and Henry's place.

The doctors at the hospital have diagnosed Amanda as having double pnuemonia and a repressed immune system. She is not fighting off the illness, not responding to medication.

I'm beginning to find out how agonizing guilt can be. The mental anguish is almost more than I can bear. A thousand times an hour I'm thinking, If only we had put Amanda into the hospital right away, instead of driving to Toronto with her. But now it's too late. ❧

*A*manda has been in a coma most of the day, and tonight at 7:00 o'clock while we were gathered around her bed, she breathed her last.

Oh, God, the agonizing pain of my aching heart is overwhelming. My body is raked raw with unfathomable heartache. I felt my faith wavering and slipping and wondered if God was really there, whether he hears our prayers.

Death is so final, so irrevocable. While there's life there's hope, they say. How true. When life is gone . . . hope is gone.

The Shadow

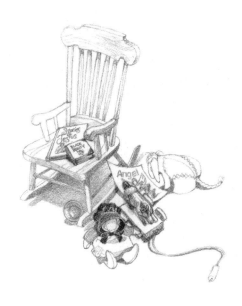

*W*hy do I try to write at a time like this? I am in a daze, feeling numb, not even able to feel pain. Writing helps me regain a feeling of control.

People have been coming and going all day. This forenoon they planned the funeral (it will be on Friday), and this afternoon they cleaned the house. They even scrubbed the walls, windows, woodwork, and doors. Tomorrow they'll prepare food.

Realizing so many people care and are helping so much has comforted me. I'm even able to see and understand what a great gain this is for Amanda, even in the midst of our loss. And that blessed hope that we'll someday be with her again sustains my spirit.

Late this afternoon, Dora came running to me and reported, "They're carrying Amanda into the house."

The innocent excitement in her voice made my throat choke up. We watched, hand in hand, as they carried the small coffin into the sitting room.

I turned my back and swallowed hard as the undertaker opened the lid. Would I be able to remain composed in front of the children? Oh, that sweet little smile on her white and still face, so serene. Those little hands that were so dear and eager to help, now so cold and still.

Nate brought the rest of the children to see Amanda,

and we stood around the coffin with bowed heads. I felt a little hand slip into mine, and Peter turned his tearstained face up to me. "That's not the real Amanda, is it?"

"No," I answered, trying to give him a reassuring smile. "The real Amanda is with Jesus. That's just the body she used to live in." ❧

January 7

*T*he other children are a big comfort to me these days, but every room of the house is full of memories of Amanda. Whenever I come across a fresh sign of her, I think of that lonely little grave—that a little girl so alive and so precious is there, now cold and still in death.

Will we never again hear her sing, "Jesus loves me this I know," in that sweet, childish voice of hers? Or hear her shriek with laughter, like she used to when Rudy tossed her up into the air?

The memories of the funeral are already hazy. I know that Emanuel Yoder and the bishop preached comforting and encouraging sermons, but I can't remember a word they said, and it bothers me considerably. I wish someone would've taken it down in shorthand and would give it to me now. ❧

January 12

*D*ora came to me, in tears this morning, and showed me a box of Amanda's beloved little

valuables, toys and odds and ends she had found in her drawer.

"Do you think we could somehow send these up to heaven so Amanda could play with them?" she asked tearfully.

I explained to her that Amanda now has treasures much better than any she had on earth, and I tucked away the little box into my drawer of keepsakes and memories. How paltry such things would seem to her now.

Tonight after I tucked the children into bed, told them a bedtime story, kissed them good-night, and was ready to tiptoe out of the room, Peter whispered, "Mam, does Jesus tuck Amanda into bed now and tell her a bedtime story?"

Sadie heard it and added, "Does Jesus kiss her good-night now?"

Dora answered the question for them in a matter-of-fact tone. "Of course he does." ❧

The numbness is wearing off, and I am beginning to feel the pain, just as when Novocain in a tooth wears off, and a toothache returns. With the pain, the feelings of guilt return. How can I ever forgive myself for taking Amanda up there to Toronto to a quack doctor?

I was the one who pushed for it, and I can't help but feel that Amanda would still be with us if we had put her into the hospital right away. The thought haunts me day and night. I've asked God many times to forgive me, and I believe he has, but the guilt is still there. How can that be?

People have been so kind and helpful. I haven't needed to cook, for friends and neighbors have been bringing in our meals, to tempt our lagging appetites. Letters and cards arrive daily, and they do help to cheer us up.

We've had encouraging visitors every day so far. Grandpa Daves and Henry and Priscilla dropped in almost daily. Allen and Polly paid us a welcome visit, and Isaac and Rosemary wrote us a comforting letter. The dear church members have been so kind and caring.

Brotherly and sisterly love is so big and so beautiful, it's no wonder heaven is a place to look forward to. What would we do without good friends like these?

Yet still the pain and guilt persist. ❧

Tonight I wrote a long letter to Polly. I thought maybe it would help me to confess to someone else, to unburden myself to another person, one who understands. She was a real friend to me in our single days, and it was a treat for me to visit her in her cute little house trimmed with blue, with lots of flower beds in the yard, and shelves of good books inside.

Memories of living in her house while I had my leg broken came crowding back, and of Grandma (Frieda's mother) living with us. Suddenly I was overwhelmed with a desire to see Grandma once again.

I wonder, are she and Amanda with each other in heaven? The thought cheers me immensely. I imagine them, walking hand in hand with Jesus, on that shining shore. For the first time since Amanda's death, I feel a measure of peace in my heart.

"He will swallow up death in victory; and the Lord God will wipe away tears from off all faces; and the rebuke of his people shall he take away from off all the earth: for the Lord has spoken it." ❧

January 31

*N*ate has been my tower of strength these days. More than once he has encouraged me to face head-on whatever I dreaded. There was such a case today.

I was invited to a quilting at Emanuel Yoders, with a carry-in dinner. They put four quilts into frames. The profits of those quilts are to go toward paying the expenses of our trip to Toronto, and the doctor and hospital bills.

I felt so humiliated—other people having to help pay for my folly. I wanted to do like the ostrich—bury my head in the sand. But, at Nate's bidding, I went, and it wasn't nearly as bad as I'd feared. I actually enjoyed the day.

But for the first time, I really understood why it is more blessed to give than to receive, like it says in Acts. To be on the receiving end takes a giving up, a swallowing of pride. "God loves a cheerful giver," and I'm sure he also loves a cheerful receiver. ❧

February 3

*B*y return mail I received a long letter from Polly. I went into my bedroom and closed the door to read it. At the top of her letter, she had copied this little poem:

Just as Thou wilt, is just what I would will;
   Give me but this, the heart to be content,
And, if my wish is thwarted, to lie still,
   Waiting till puzzle and till pain are spent
And the sweet thing made plain, which the Lord meant.
                   —*Susan Coolidge*

I'll also copy part of her letter that moved me to tears, an avalanche of them.

"Reading between the lines of your letter, I see that you're assured of God's forgiveness, but that you've never really forgiven yourself. You're still carrying around the burden of your guilt. Don't you think, in God's sight, it might be just as wrong for you to refuse to forgive yourself as it would be to refuse to forgive someone else?

"Next you'll make yourself sick, for the human body and mind wasn't meant to carry such a burden. It's all right to cry, to grieve out the pain. But if you've forgiven yourself, your tears will be cleansing and healing tears, instead of a festering wound of remorse. God can redeem even our mistakes and make something good and beautiful out of them. Only trust God. 'In all your ways acknowledge God, and he shall direct your paths.' "

Then and there I confessed my sin to God, the sin of refusing to forgive myself. I cried for a long time, and it was true, they were tears of cleansing, healing, and thankfulness. I opened the Bible to Psalm 51 and read: "Purge me with hyssop, and I shall be clean: wash me, and I shall be whiter than snow."

Lord, I feel as if I've already been purged with hyssop, and washed clean, and my heart overflows with thanksgiving.

"Create in me a clean heart, O God; and renew a right spirit within me. Cast me not away from your presence; and take not your Holy Spirit from me. Restore unto me the joy of your salvation; and uphold me with your free spirit."

I can't believe how different I feel. For the first time since Amanda's death, I sense God's presence. In his presence is fullness of joy! ❦

February 24

A joyous heart! Today Dora threw her arms around me, and exclaimed, "Mam, you're happy again!"

"Oh, yes," I told her. "Just think how happy Amanda must be. I'm sure she'd want us to be happy, too."

It's good to feel an interest in the mundane things of life once again, as in my work. In life, whatever would we do without our daily work giving us a sense of having accomplished something? Once again I enjoy a good meal and happily watch the snow drifting down and the birds busy at the feeder. God gives us all things richly to enjoy.

That tense, weepy feeling is gone, and I am rejoicing. When Nate came in and heard me singing, he commented, "The sun is shining again in our home."

I suppose it's true that the mother in a home creates the atmosphere. If she is grumpy, everyone else is, too. If she is joyous, the others begin to feel happy, too. ❧

March 9

*I*s there a sweeter sound in the morning than waking to the chorus of birdsong? Or the patter of little feet as Sadie and Crist come downstairs and through the hall? It reminds me of the poem "Pitty Pat and Tippy Toe." I love to hear the banty roosters crowing, welcoming the sun. Best of all, is the sound of Nate singing as he herds in the cows. Precious morning sounds. We have so much to be thankful for. ❧

May 10

*R*udy came in this morning with shining eyes and said there's something in the barn for us all to see. We eagerly followed him outdoors, and

there in the box stall, with protective Mama Nellie hovering over it, was a wobbly new baby colt. Nellie nuzzled her colt and let out a nicker of joy, and the colt responded with a high, baby whinny.

Oh, the miracle of birth and new life on the farm. It was quite exciting for the children, and for a while they could talk of nothing else. On the way back into the house, I spied a robin's nest in the spirea bush, and the bleeding heart bush was in bloom. The garden is as pretty as a picture with its neat rows of vegetables and the blossoming wild cherry trees along the creek—it's almost too beautiful. I could weep with the wonder of it—tears of awe and joy. Truly the goodness of God is declared in his handiwork. 🐾

I've been thinking that I'll have to let Barbianne go this fall. I won't have any excuse anymore to have a *Maud.* My baby is over two, and the children are all healthy.

Barbianne and Rudy have me puzzled. There is no more teasing going on between them, only a deep tenderness, comradeship, and a love-light in their eyes, yet they aren't dating each other. I've been told that lots of boys have asked Barbianne for dates, but she turns them down flat. I wonder what she and Rudy are waiting for. ❧

*G*randpa Daves and Henry and Priscilla were here for supper, and we had an old-time gabfest once again. Over the winter, our visiting was rather strained by our sorrow, so it was good to hear Grandpa Dave launch into one of his stories once again.

Little Miriam was the center of attraction, though, another "grandchild," for Dave and Annie, and everyone wanted to hold her. She looked like a little doll with her puffed sleeves and light colored dress, big dark eyes and little *Bobbies* (banded loops of hair).

Sometimes I wonder if Priscilla isn't overdoing it a bit by dressing her up like that. But I'm afraid her feelings would be hurt if I'd mention it to her. Those smocked dresses she wears for everyday are definitely too fancy, too, but I guess nothing is too good for her little darling. Every stitch is put in with meticulous care, I'm sure.

Tonight after our company had left, a car drove in, and here was Gloria Graham, with Kitty Kat. She was visibly upset about something as she walked in the door without knocking, an agitated look on her face.

"George [her husband] is the most hard-hearted man I ever saw!" she complained tearfully, putting Kitty Kat down on the settee cushion. "Tonight he told me, 'Either that cat goes, or I go!' That's his ultimatum, and he won't back down!"

"You mean you have to choose between him and the cat?" I gasped.

"That's right! He's cruel, he's unfair, he's selfish!" she ranted. "He's jealous, that's what he is. I ought to teach him a lesson, that's what."

"So?" We heard a cool, masculine voice from outside the screen door. There stood George, looking into the kitchen. "I followed you down here," he stated calmly. "If that's the way you feel about me, I'm leaving. I can't put up with that cat any longer.

"At night if I roll over in bed, your precious cat is disturbed. When I sit down for a snack, there comes your cat, sniffing and pawing into my food, and you won't let me lift a finger to make her move. When I sit down to read the paper, she mews for attention until I have to leave the room.

"I'm sick of it. So this is good-bye. If you ever change your mind, give me a call. I'll be at a hotel in town!" He turned, walked out to his car, and drove off.

"See what I mean?" Gloria gasped, in a weak, trembling voice. "He's jealous." But the fire had gone out of her voice and manner, and soon she left, too.

"Whose side are you on?" Nate asked me later, after I'd told him the story.

"I sympathize with George, of course," I replied. "I think Gloria ought to be willing to give up the cat for his sake. Remember how you gave up hunting and fishing for me, when you married me?"

"Well, if you were good enough to give up Allen Keim for me, I guess I could do that much," he teased.

To myself I thought, I might not have given him up, if I'd have loved him half as much as Gloria loves that cat. 🐾

July 17

A peaceful Sunday evening on lawn chairs under the trees, the children romping with Cocky and catching fireflies. Heat lightning flashed in the west, and there was an occasional low, faraway rumble of thunder.

"I'm worried about Henry," Nate shared, shattering the peacefulness of the evening.

"Why? What's wrong?" I jerked to attention.

"You probably noticed that he wasn't at church today."

"I guess I did, but I didn't give it much thought. Maybe he was sick."

"No, preacher Emanuel said that when he passed there on the way to church, Henry was out in the yard, practicing pitching quoits. Didn't Priscilla say anything about it?"

"No, she didn't. Maybe he had the 'summer complaint,' " I defended Henry. "Maybe he didn't want to disturb the services by running out all the time."

"Ha!" Nate laughed. "If he would've had that, he wouldn't have had the strength to pitch quoits either."

"Well, let's give him the benefit of the doubt and not

blame him for something we're not sure of."

I felt stubborn and was beginning to feel upset. I so much wanted Henry to make good. ❦

July 20

*G*loria Graham came tonight again, with Kitty Kat, and by this time she was ready to give up her will. "I miss Georgie so much," she blubbered. "Would you be kind enough to give Kitty Kat a home? Then I could come out once a day to see her."

"But . . . but, did you forget how it went the other time?" I sputtered. "Did you forget how upset you were when the cat got lost?" I wanted to rub it in and add, And how you threatened to sue us? But I didn't dare.

"I know, I know," Gloria responded meekly. "But then she was just hiding in the barn. She was all right, weren't you Kitty Kat, darling?" she stroked the cat's magnificent white coat.

I decided to put her off. "First let me talk to Nate about it."

"Okay, that's fine," Gloria agreed. "I'll be back tomorrow morning to see what you've decided."

Later, when Nate came in, I told him about it and added, "You can choose between me and Kitty Kat!" ❦

July 31

*T*onight we and Grandpa Daves drove over to see Priscilla and Henry. Again this morning, Henry didn't show up for church services. With tears in her eyes, Priscilla told me that she hitched up the horse by herself and came alone with little Miriam. I wanted to ask her more, but not with so many eyes watching us. She left right after dinner, and at her request, we let Dora go home with her.

As Grandma Annie and I strolled up the walk to Henry's house tonight, we heard loud voices, as if they were in a heated argument. Then suddenly all was quiet, and in a moment Priscilla came to the door.

"Hello! What a nice surprise this is!" she exclaimed cheerfully enough. "Come in!" She held the door open wide. Henry brushed past us without as much as a hello and joined Grandpa Dave and Nate at the railing where they were tying the horses.

"Dora and Miriam are out in the backyard, playing with Kitty Kat." Priscilla seemed unperturbed. "Why don't we go and join them?"

"Kitty Kat?" I echoed. "Did Gloria ask you to give him a home?"

Priscilla nodded. "Yes, she did, and it didn't take me long to decide. I simply adore cats, especially Persians."

"Well!" I returned, "I'm glad Gloria found a home for her, but . . . I just hope nothing happens to her."

"I know. I remember how she threatened to sue you. But Henry and I aren't worried about that. We have liability insurance."

"So you're ready for trouble," I responded. "I guess our *Ordnung* (order, rules) does allow that now."

Priscilla shrugged her shoulders indifferently and changed the subject.

Dora came running to meet us, followed by Kitty Kat.

"I'm teaching Miriam to walk," she bubbled enthusiastically.

She ran back to Baby Miriam and led her over to us. Miriam was wearing a short dress with ruffled sleeves and a polka-dotted bonnet, which made her look almost exactly like an *englisch* (non-Amish) baby. I stifled a gasp, and Grandma muttered, "Tsk, tsk." If Priscilla heard it, she pretended not to notice.

Twice Grandma Annie steered the conversation to Henry's absence from church, and each time Priscilla quickly changed the subject. Grandpa Dave and Nate didn't fare any better. Henry seemed quiet and withdrawn and didn't say much. ❧

August 17

A long day. We canned over fifty quarts of chowchow. We have a satisfying feeling as we look over the rows of jars of colorful vegetables—lima beans, corn, peppers, pickles, carrots, and string beans. It's a lot of work, but it's worth it. Now, next winter when the snow is flying outside, we can go to the cellar for a jar of delicious chowchow.

Grandpa Dave and Annie helped, and Barbianne and Rudy. We also sent word to Henry and Priscilla, but they didn't show up. Last Sunday Henry was at church services, but Priscilla and Miriam weren't there. Tongues are starting to wag, and we are becoming increasingly worried about those two.

I keep reminding myself, Why worry when you can pray? If only they would confide in us or the ministers, maybe we could help them. But they're downright uncommunicative.

Emanuel Yoder told us that last Thursday an unfamiliar looking car was parked in Henry's drive all day. Dora spent a few days there again, in the beginning of the week, and she said that Henry and Priscilla are now using the electricity in the house.

Earlier, they had been careful to use the gas lanterns instead of the electric lights, and to pump the water by hand instead of using the electric pump and pressure system. They had been strict in keeping the rules of the church and respecting the *Ordnung*, and they seemed happy and satisfied.

Why this now? Surely they realize that they, on bended knees, promised to obey the rules of the church, and that it is sin for them not to keep the *Ordnung*. I can't understand it, and my heart bleeds for them.

Oh, God, give them wisdom and understanding. Help them to realize that "there is a way which seems right to people, but the end thereof is the way of death." ❧

September 1

I've been having lonesome thoughts of Amanda all day. Maybe it was because I had such a vivid dream about her last night. I dreamed I was busy in the kitchen when I heard Amanda laughing outside, in that clear, sweet voice of hers. I dashed out—I just had to find her, at least to get a glimpse of her. But she was nowhere to be seen.

I woke with tears streaming down my cheeks. Then all

day I kept seeing Amanda in my mind's eye.

I saw her sitting in the lush green grass down by the creek, picking a bouquet of forget-me-nots for me. I saw her sitting on the porch steps, with her arms full of kittens, talking softly and crooning to them as she used to do. I saw her on the swing, clutching her beloved little rag doll that Grandma Annie gave her for Christmas a few years ago, and whispering her little-girl secrets to it.

I felt lonely and weepy until I once again came to the confidence that Amanda is with Jesus, and how gloriously happy she must be! The memories of her comforted me then, and I thanked God for allowing me to have her for three years and nine months. Although I have no photographs of her, I'll never forget her sweet little face. And I am blessed indeed, to be the mother of a "little angel." ❧

September 6

*A*t last the long-awaited day arrived: Dora's first day of school! She was enthusiastic, too excited to eat breakfast.

I had some qualms about sending such a little girl off alone to a big public school. But I consoled myself with the thought that Dora is spunky and can handle it. I had been hoping we'd have our Amish school ready for this district by fall, but it was not to be. By next fall we will have it, though, and I don't think one year of public school is going to do a little first-grade Amish girl any harm.

The parochial school at the north end of the district was full this year. For a while we were considering doing home schooling, but since Nate and I both went to public school, we decided it this way, much to Grandpa Dave's chagrin.

"Don't you realize how much public schools have changed in forty years?" he scolded. "You're asking for trouble, to my way of thinking. They probably teach that humans descended from monkeys, and they're not allowed to have Bible reading and prayer.

"The girls wear boys' clothes, and the boys have long hair like the girls. They're not allowed to discipline by spanking, and they say the children are quite unruly. You're making a big mistake, let me tell you."

This all added to my misgivings when the big yellow school bus chugged up the road. I had offered to walk out to the end of the lane with Dora, but she was fiercely independent and declined my offer. She looked so small, carrying her new lunch box and wearing her new bonnet, green dress, and black apron.

My thoughts were with her all day as I went about my work, wondering and worrying. Finally, at 3:30 the big yellow school bus stopped again at the end of the lane, and Dora came skipping in swinging her bonnet by the strings. I could see, by the smile on her face, that it had been a good day for her.

"Well, what did you learn at school today?" Nate teased her.

"I learned that I'm the only Amish girl in my class," she replied, half proudly. Then she added, "Say, Dad, what does 'peculiar' mean? Are we peculiar? A boy in my class said we are."

"I guess that's what we're supposed to be," Nate replied mildly.

Running through my mind was a verse from Titus: "Our Savior Jesus Christ . . . gave himself for us, that he might redeem us from all iniquity, and purify unto himself a peculiar people, zealous of good works." 🍂

We were canning grape juice, and the kitchen was filling with the wonderful aroma of grapes cooking. Barbianne was up on the stepladder by the grapevine, cutting down a dishpanful of grapes, when I heard a clattering sound.

For a moment I thought the ladder had fallen over, but then I saw a horse and buggy come tearing in the lane, without a driver. With a swift intake of breath, I ran outside. It was Henry's black horse with the white star on his forehead.

"Oh, no, not again!" I wailed. That had happened once before. Surely he hadn't neglected to tie him this time! Nate and Rudy were there right away, and Barbianne and I joined them as they tied the horse.

"I don't think he ran far. See, he's not breathing hard," observed Nate. "Rudy, why don't you jump on the scooter and go out the road to see if you can find anyone."

"Look!" Peter cried. "The horse's leg is bleeding."

A moment later Sadie called out, "Here come Priscilla and baby Miriam!"

Priscilla's face looked like a storm as she walked in the lane and over to her rig. "Never again!" she declared fiercely. "That does it. I've had it!"

"What happened?" I asked weakly.

"Coming down the hill, past the trailer, the horse slipped and fell." Her lips were trembling. "I got out with the reins, and just then he jumped up and took off. I had Miriam in my arms, too, and I couldn't hold him back."

"All's well that ends well," Nate assured her. "We can all be thankful that you didn't leave Miriam sitting on the seat. She might've been thrown off and hurt when the horse went around the corner."

Priscilla turned and without a word went into the house.

"Why do you think she said what she did?" I whispered worriedly to Nate. "Do you think she meant it?"

"No, no, she was just all upset. Go in and comfort her the best you can."

When I got into the house, Priscilla had thrown off her bonnet and stood by the window. "Please don't tell Henry," she implored. "I'm afraid this is the last straw." She blinked away a few tears.

"I see no reason why he has to know. Your horse only had a few scratches on his leg. Nate is putting some ointment on it, and he should be good as new by the time you're ready to go home. God had his protecting hand over you, and we should thank him and feel grateful. Do you want to make a few grape pies for lunch?"

Priscilla donned her baking apron and began to mix pie dough. "You're always so cheerful and contented," she observed wistfully. "I feel so mixed up and out of fellowship with God. He seems far away, not hearing my prayers anymore." She again whisked away tears on her cheek.

"I believe I know what you're going through," I consoled her. "A big shadow fell over me after Amanda's death. I felt so guilty and in despair, and God seemed far away."

"What?" Priscilla exclaimed, shocked. "I never would've guessed it. You seemed so surrendered. Other people talked about it, too."

I laughed. "Things aren't always as they appear to be. But I surely thought the turmoil and the struggles in my heart would've been visible on my face."

"How did you . . . ah . . . when did you start feeling better?" Priscilla wondered.

I pondered this a bit, then replied, "I think the best thing to do is to confide in someone else, an understanding friend, who can help you get things in their proper perspective. I wrote a long letter to Polly, and she wrote back, and her letter was a big help to me.

"Nate and I have been telling each other that we wish you and Henry would confide in someone about your problems. We wondered whether or not we should bring up the subject, but we didn't want to 'rush in where angels fear to tread' [Pope]."

Priscilla had to smile a bit at this. "Maybe it's stubbornness," she shared meekly, "but we haven't really felt like confiding in anyone just yet. We were so happy . . . and now. . . ." Her voice broke off, and she resolutely pinched her mouth shut and was silent.

My heart ached for her. I didn't want to sound preachy. I wanted to say, "Take it to the Lord in prayer" [Scriven] and trust him to work it all out for your good. But I was afraid it would sound too glib to Priscilla. Besides, they were going to have to learn to give up their own selfish will before God's will could be done. ❧

Tonight when Dora came home from school, she flung her bonnet into a corner, raced up the stairs, and slammed the door to her room. The sound of stormy weeping floated downstairs. Wearily, I trudged up the stairs after her, dreading to hear what she had to say.

"I hate school!" She was angry. "I'm not going back again! You can teach me the lessons here at home."

"Why, what happened? Doesn't the teacher treat you fairly?"

"Yes, the teacher is nice, but it's those stupid children I don't like. They won't play with me, and they called me names." She burst into a fresh round of sobbing.

"Well, change into your everyday clothes and come downstairs. Help me mix chocolate chip cookies, and we'll talk about it. The other children are outside with Barbianne."

She told me all about it as she stirred the shortening and sugar and mixed in the eggs with the big wooden spoon. Jimmy, a boy in her class, had called her "the bonnet girl," and soon all the rest were calling her "bonnie girl." She again wiped away a few tears as she told it.

"Don't you know what *bonnie* means?" I asked.

She shook her head no.

"It means 'handsome' or 'pretty,' and I'd be glad if someone called me bonnie."

"Does it really?" Her eyes lit up. "I thought they meant I look like a *Haas* (bunny)."

We laughed together then, and she was her happy self again. ❧

A clear, crisp, windy day. The corn for the silo is cut on our farm now, and I can look over the valley again. I love to see green cornfields growing in the summertime, but in the fall when the stalks are brown and dead, I'm glad to see it cut. It gives a sense of openness and spaciousness.

We're finding out that Peter is quite a strong-willed little fellow. Lately, he has been taking more spankings than all the others combined. This morning, as soon as the milking was done, Nate and Rudy got ready to go silo filling over on the Foster farm, and Peter thought he just had to go along.

Nate told him he couldn't, so when Nate wasn't looking, Peter climbed on the back of the wagon and lay down flat, thinking he wouldn't be seen. It probably would have worked, had it not been for his straw hat. Nate administered a spanking before they left, and Peter came in to me, pouting.

He was still feeling rebellious and announced loudly, "I'm going to run away!" His lower lip stuck out like a bird's perch.

"Oh? Where are you going to run to?"

"To the woods, and Cocky's going with me."

His tear-stained little face looked so defiantly funny that I turned away to hide a smile.

"What would you have to eat, in the woods?"

He pondered this awhile. "I'm going to take lots of sandwiches along. And I'll drink water out of the spring."

"What would you do if a rabid fox would come and bite you?"

Peter's eyes grew big. He didn't have an answer to that, and he soon ran off to play, apparently having forgotten about running away.

Later in the morning, Sadie came in, weeping heart-brokenly and carefully holding her precious "momie doll," as she calls it. "Peter tore my dollie's arm off," she sobbed. "Please go and spank him good!"

I called Peter in, and he sulkily stood in the doorway. "Why did you do it?" I asked him sorrowfully.

" 'Cause she didn't listen to me!" he shot back. "I made myself a farm and was filling silo, and I told her she couldn't drive in my fields. But she drove right through them anyway with her dolly stroller!"

After I had settled that quarrel, disciplined Peter, and had a heart-to-heart talk with him, they played peacefully for awhile. When I was sewing the rag doll's arm back on, I again heard the sound of quarreling and crying—this time it was Peter and Crist. It seemed like I was settling quarrels all day.

When Dora came home from school, she was on the verge of tears. I thought, This is why mothers get gray.

I followed Dora to her room, and she told me tearfully, "The other children don't want to play with me at recess, and I don't like to play by myself."

I encouraged her to be friendly and kind, and I promised that after they got to know her better, she would have lots of friends. But she still had an unhappy evening.

This evening when Grandpa Daves stopped in for a few minutes, I poured out my tale of woe to Grandma. She had an instant remedy for both my problems. Dora should be taken out of public school, and the little ones should be given a dose of pinworm medicine.

Somehow, neither of those remedies appealed to me. I keep thinking, *"ball wollt's besser geh* (soon it will go better)."

It is 10:00 p.m., and Nate and Rudy are still not home. Maybe Nate partly meant it when he said we'd work twenty-four hours a day and half the night. Barbianne and I did the chores alone, then worked in the garden until bedtime. Now the children are in bed, and all is quiet and peaceful.

Outside a silvery moon hangs over the treetops, and millions of twinkling stars shine in the sky. I wonder why I don't oftener take the time to look at the stars and think of their Creator. It's such an awesome, dazzling display.

I sit here at the window, musing and reminiscing, my thoughts traveling from one subject to the next. Someday I'll look back with nostalgia and longing to these busy, happy times, even to childish quarrels and school problems.

Thank you, Father, for my babies. Help me to love and appreciate them while I have them, and never take them for granted. ❧

September 27

Another long day of silo filling for Nate and Rudy. I love this time of year, yet I'll heave a sigh of relief when they're finished. I don't like when they work so late, and besides, it's dangerous.

This morning I decided to take Peter and walk over to spend the day with Priscilla. We haven't heard from them for awhile. Other than praying for them, we don't know what we could do for them.

As we walked past the trailer, I noticed the windows had been cleaned and new curtains put up. Since the corn is off, I had several times seen a car parked in the drive. Now, sure enough, it looked like someone had moved in.

I was just thinking, I sure hope they will be nicer folks than the former occupants, when the front door opened, and a lady walked out and got into the car. She drove past us and cheerily waved her hand. Then as if on impulse, stopped and backed up, opened the window, and called out, "Hi! May I give you a lift? I'm going your way, and you won't have to walk."

She looked decent and friendly, and I decided to trust her. We got on the front seat beside her, and she introduced herself. "My name is Pamela Styer, and I just moved into this trailer. I suppose you're one of my closet neighbors, the Masts, right?"

"Yes, I'm Miriam, and this is Peter."

"Your farm is a real hideaway," she commented wistfully. "I'd love living among the trees like that. I just moved out here to the country for some peace and quiet to write my novel. But I didn't realize it would be quite this lonely. Mind if I come over sometimes, when it gets too bad?"

"You're welcome to come anytime," I told her, for politeness' sake.

She had her hair cut in a pageboy style, was wearing a pantsuit, and had on gold earrings. "What kind of a novel are you writing?" I asked, my curiosity getting the better of me.

"It has its setting in the Civil War days. The people then lived much the way you Amish people do, and that's another reason I'd like to get to know you better. When it's finished, I'll give you a copy to read."

I had serious doubts that we lived as people did in Civil War days, but said nothing. Pamela was quite talkative, and before we arrived at Priscilla's house, I had learned that Pamela was nearly the same age as I, she had two grown children (both married and living in other states), and her husband was overseas doing some job for the company that employed him.

"I'm so glad I learned to know you." Pamela graciously stopped the car at Priscilla's front gate. "Please feel free to come over any time to use my telephone, or if you need a lift to go shopping, or whatever, I'll be glad to take you."

I thanked her for the offer, and she waved gaily as she drove off.

Priscilla was out in the backyard, trimming around her marigold and zinnia bed, with Miriam in the stroller beside her. She seemed genuinely glad to see me. "What a lovely surprise! Come on in, and we'll work on my quilt while we talk."

Peter was already playing with Miriam and had her laughing out loud.

"You've no idea how lonely it can get when your husband is gone all day, day after day," Priscilla went on. "You farm wives have it made."

"What!" I pretended to be shocked. "When it's this busy, I hardly see my farmer, from before dawn, to around 11:00 p.m. Henry comes home at 6:00, and then you have five hours of togetherness, don't you?"

Priscilla looked a bit sheepish. "Well . . . if you put it that way, it does seem. . . ."

"I know what you mean, though," I quickly added. "Farmers aren't always that busy. I can imagine you'd be lonely during the day."

In the sitting room Priscilla had a dahlia quilt in the frame, and she went to her sewing basket to get me a thimble and a needle. I glanced around the room. There on the sideboard was a lovely framed photograph of little Miriam, and again, she was dressed so fancy, she looked like a little *englisch* girl. My heart sank. Having a photograph of oneself or one's child displayed like that was strictly forbidden in the *Ordnung* (rules).

Should I mention it to Priscilla or pretend I hadn't seen it? Surely she knew, and Henry knew well enough, that they were transgressing by having things which they had promised to deny themselves when they joined the church.

Priscilla breezed back into the sitting room with the needle and thimble and was chattering away about this and that. I began to quilt, and while I had my back turned, I heard her opening and closing a drawer. The next time I looked, the photograph wasn't there anymore. So! At least Priscilla had the grace to be ashamed of it, then. Doesn't she realize that God sees everything?

As we quilted, Priscilla was talking away at a great rate, jumping from one subject to the next. "Did you hear about the midwife that's starting to do home deliveries in this area? I think I'd like to try her next time."

"No, I hadn't heard. I guess I sort of grew out of that. I won't be needing a midwife anymore."

"Don't talk too soon," Priscilla teased. "You're not forty-nine yet. Didn't you hear about Abner Emma [Abner's wife]? She's forty-nine and due in January."

"But she has four grandchildren already! Surely that's not true!"

"Yes, I know it's true. Her sister told me. She said she didn't know whether to laugh or to cry."

The day passed quickly with such chatter, for Priscilla kept a conversation going constantly, maybe to keep me from talking about something she didn't want to hear. She served a casserole dish of *Yummasetti* for lunch, and for dessert we had cherry cream cheese delight. Both were delicious!

Peter kept Miriam entertained, and they both napped for several hours. At least he didn't quarrel with her. Maybe it did him good, too, to get away for a day. I enjoyed the day, yet I didn't have a happy, refreshed feeling when I came home. It wasn't hard to figure out why. 🍂

October 3

*T*he God I know is a God close by,
Not seated on a throne in far-off sky,
He is here on this earth, reflected in trees,
In mountains, in flower, in sweet summer breeze,
In ocean's grandeur, in plain's delight,
In noontide glare, and in stilly night,
In children's prattle, in manhood's prime,
Since the birth of worlds until end of time,
For the God I know with a thought that's free
Is the God of Love, found in you and me.
                              —Carleton Everett Knox

This poem reminded me of our trip to Toronto, and how I didn't feel close to God because I couldn't see his handiwork. To me, living out in the countryside is a wonderful blessing. I know that God is not closer to Christians here than he is to his children in cities, but I'm afraid I could never feel at home living in a city.

This morning we had our first killing frost, which froze the tender flowers black. Later the sun came out nice and warm, though, and I spent the day working outside, pulling out the frozen impatiens, coleuses, and begonias, and loading them on the wheelbarrow.

Peter and Sadie (and even little Crist) helped, loading whatever they could on their little red wagon. My heart ached for awhile when I remembered that last year Amanda had helped with this job, and now she was no longer with us. I have to accept that fact over and over—it's not something that can be done once for all.

This afternoon we pulled the tomato vines and pepper stalks out of the garden, and Nate chopped down the last round of sweet corn. Then he hitched Nellie to the hand cultivator and tilled it. Her colt is growing so fast it's almost unbelievable—soon he'll be helping with the farm work, too.

When Dora got off the school bus, she came running straight over to me, looking gloriously happy. "Mam, I have a friend!" She was enthusiastic, her eyes shining. "Her name is Cheryl. She sat beside me at lunchtime, and we played together at first and last recess!"

"That's nice." I was smiling. "Didn't I tell you that's the way it would go?"

"She's going to invite me to her house sometime, to stay for the night," Dora went on eagerly. She swung her bonnet round and round by the strings as she talked. "I can hardly wait. She said she likes me better than any other friend she ever had, and she's going to give me one of her dolls. She has six of them."

Dora could talk of nothing else all evening. She dawdled and fussed so much, while washing the supper dishes, that I finally had to give her a time limit. When she packed her lunch for tomorrow, she asked if she could put in an extra cupcake for Cheryl.

For Dora's sake, I hope the friendship lasts, now that at last she's found a bosom friend. ❦

October 11

*F*inally, brethren, whatsoever things are true, whatsoever things are honest, whatsoever things are just, whatsoever things are pure, whatsoever things are lovely, whatsoever things are of good report, . . . think on these things."

We had our *Faschtdaag* (fast day) today. We spent the forenoon at home, in Bible reading, prayer, and meditation. Then this afternoon we visited some shut-ins.

Grandpa Daves stopped in tonight for a few minutes. They said the ministers went to see Henry and Priscilla, to see if they can get them to line up with the *Ordnung* (church order, rules), so they can participate in the communion services.

Let us pray earnestly for them. They are confused and floundering in the faith. We had so hoped they would be steadfast, upbuilding members of the church, strong pillars for righteousness, and a good example to the oncoming generation.

After Daves had left, we went for a walk way back to the *Kette-Schtecke* (swinging bridge). It had been a damp, rainy day, then tonight the wind swung to the west, and the clouds blew away. Wild geese flew high overhead, honking their way southward.

Peter picked up a wooly caterpillar, and its coat was a dark brown color, which is supposed to mean it will be a long, cold winter. Squirrels scampered busily among the trees, gathering shellbarks and other nuts for winter. Nate searched for arrowheads, and the children gathered bright-colored leaves.

Black-capped chickadees, my favorite of the feathered friends, flitted among the trees. I cherish times of family togetherness like these, but feel so conscious of the fact that one is missing, that the family circle is no longer complete. "Will the circle be unbroken" by and by? ❧

October 23, Sunday evening

*W*e attended communion services at Emanuel Yoders. Henry and Priscilla did not take part—they were not even there. My heart aches for them. Last week Priscilla confided in Grandma Annie, "We are torn with indecision, and we cannot agree with each other in the smallest matters anymore. The joy has gone out of life. There is no peace, no satisfying communion and fellowship."

They need encouragement and prayer, but the battle is theirs. They must crucify self with the affections and lusts and give up their own will.

Lately I've been wondering a lot about Barbianne and Rudy. He takes her to the singings regularly (but there was no singing tonight because this was communion Sunday).

I'm quite sure now that they are in love with each other. But as usual they are secretive about it. This is Barbianne's last month here. Maybe they'll start dating then. I can hardly wait to see what develops between the two of them. 🌿

*D*ora is happily excited these days. She comes home from school full of stories about her new friend, Cheryl.

"Cheryl likes my new bonnet," she bubbled happily one evening. "Could you make her one like it, too? She'd like to have one."

The next day it was an apron. "Cheryl would like to have a black apron just like mine."

Then on Monday evening she came home, burst breathless and panting into the parlor where we were busy housecleaning, and reported, "Mam, guess what! Cheryl invited me to go home from school with her and spend the night there! Please, oh please, say yes. I want to go so much!" She was jumping up and down, first on one foot, then on the other.

"I'll talk it over with Dad," I promised. "Go and change your clothes. Then you can help to wash the woodwork." She raced up the stairs and was down again in five minutes and out the door to tell Nate about it. Then she came back and began energetically scrubbing the baseboards and doors.

Nate and I decided to let her go. He has known Cheryl's dad for years; in fact, Nate went to school with him. They live close to town, and he works at the feed mill.

When she went to bed, Dora could hardly settle down enough to go to sleep. In the morning she was the first one up, too stirred up to eat breakfast. "I can't believe my wish is really coming true," she mused as I combed her hair and made her bob. Her dark eyes sparkled with happiness.

"Are you sure you won't get homesick and run home in the dark, like you did from Priscilla's house once?" I teased.

Dora stamped her foot indignantly. "Of course I won't! I'm a lot older now. I was just a baby then, but I'm a scholar now."

Just before she disappeared into the school bus, she waved and called, "See you tomorrow," in a grown-up tone of voice.

I felt bereft all day, especially at 3:30, when the school bus passed and no Dora got off. I commented to Nate. "We can keep our children safe and sheltered only so long, and then they must go out into the world and make their own way and their own decisions. Letting go of them is the hard part."

He answered with a Scripture verse, "Train up a child in the way which he should go, and when he is old he will not depart from it."

On Wednesday at 3:30, Dora came running in the lane at top speed. "Guess what!" she bubbled. "We ate supper at a restaurant, and we had pizza and milkshakes. Then we went back to Cheryl's house, and they have a TV set! We watched TV all evening until 10:00 o'clock. It's neat! You should just see it! And we listened to the radio when we were in bed.

"Cheryl's mom gave me money to buy my lunch, so we didn't need to pack lunch. I loved it there, and she's going to invite me again sometime. I can hardly wait!"

Later that evening Nate and I talked it over and decided that once was enough. We hadn't thought about them watching TV and listening to the radio. With all the violence and sinful behavior they can see on TV, it definitely is a harmful influence. We don't want her exposed to it again. Ꮏ

November 6

*E*manuel Yoder brought us an inspiring, soul-stirring sermon at church at Abner K.'s yesterday. I guess seeing is believing—it sure looks like it's true what Priscilla said about Abner K. Emma (wife of Abner K.). Her youngest is six years old, and now there are signs of an addition to the family yet at age forty-nine!

However, here is the big surprise! After the church services were over, the bishop announced the names of the couples wishing this fall to step into the bonds of holy matrimony with each other. The first couple to be named were Rudy and Barbianne!

I gasped out loud, and by the sound of it, I surely wasn't the only one. Several people confessed to me that they nearly fell off the bench. They had done such a good job of keeping it a secret that no one suspected. Their special day is November 24, Thanksgiving Day, and our whole family is invited.

Barbianne will be going home now, to get ready for her wedding. Then they'll do their *Hochzeit* (newlywed) visiting over the winter. Come spring, they'll be renting the Foster farm and moving there. I'm so glad we'll have them as neighbors.

Just today Rudy asked if they could rent it, and Nate decided to let them have it. That way he won't be so busy, and we won't need a full-time *Gnecht* (hired man). We had such a productive year that he feels we'll be able to make it financially, even though he just rents it out.

I like to think that God blessed him for his willingness to confess and make things right about paying his income tax. "He who confesses and forsakes sin finds mercy."

In spite of our setback with doctor and hospital bills, and our loss of Amanda, I feel we've been richly and wondrously blessed. Thank-you, Father, and help us to never take your marvelous blessings for granted. ❦

November 10

*H*ow few there are who would thus dare to address God each night: Lord, deal with me tomorrow as I have this day dealt with others . . . those to whom I was harsh, and from malice, or to show my own superiority, exposed their failings; others, to whom, from pride or dislike, I refused to speak—one I have avoided, another I cannot like because she displeases me; I will not forgive—to whom I will not show any kindness. And let us not forget, that sooner or later, God will do unto us even as we have done unto them" (*Gold Dust* translated from *Paillettes d'or*).

This is a sobering thought. Do we really "do unto others as [we] would have them do unto [us]"? Do we repeat a piece of gossip that we wouldn't want anyone to say about us? Do we interpret kindly, or judge harshly?

Jesus says, "The King shall answer and say unto them,

Verily, I say unto you, Inasmuch as you have done it unto the least of these my brothers and sisters, you have done it unto me." The least of these! If we do an unkindness to one of the least of these, we do it unto Jesus. Who are "the least of these"? One who has fallen into sin, or a scandal? One who has only one talent instead of ten?

If Jesus came to our house to visit today, wouldn't we treat him with great kindness and respect? Yet if a poor beggar came, like Lazarus, in whatever way we would treat him, we would be treating Jesus.

Today we had a welcome letter from Isaac and Rosemary in Minnesota. I am getting more and more *glushtich* (eager) to go and visit them! The children are growing out of their babyhood, and Amanda is "safe in the arms of Jesus" (Crosby).

I guess we should have gone on the trip while Barbianne was still here to babysit, but if Nate gives his consent, we could work it out somehow. Maybe Sadie and Crist could stay with Rudy and Barbianne, and we could take Dora and Peter along. But it's still only in the dream stage.

Pamela Styer was here tonight for milk, and she stayed and chatted awhile. She's interested in learning to quilt, and she admired my broken-star quilt I had in the frame. She's a friendly, interesting person, and she doesn't seem to "look down her nose" at the plain people, nor consider herself a cut above them. It wouldn't be hard to become good friends with her. ❧

We're still having warm, Indian-summer days, and I love to walk along the creek and watch the golden leaves sailing down, gently dropping into the water, and drifting downstream. The chrysanthemums are at their loveliest, with colors of wine red, yellow, and lavender—the only flowers that haven't frozen yet.

Ever since Dora spent the night at Cheryl's place, she's been begging to be allowed to invite Cheryl here for the night. Finally, on Monday, we gave our consent, for we'd like to meet this wonderful little girl, too. On Tuesday she invited Cheryl. Happily for Dora, Cheryl's mom said yes.

I had to laugh at Dora when she exclaimed, "I'm so happy, I think I might explode!" She flew around, sweeping the floor, scrubbing, wiping fingerprints, straightening up the house, and mixing cookie dough. She mercilessly bossed Peter, Sadie, and Crist around (is that the way I do when I'm worked up about something, or where did she learn that?). She even told Nate to clean up the cow stable, for Cheryl wants to go out and look at the cows.

On Wednesday she got off the bus here, and Dora proudly brought her in. She's a pretty chubby little girl with bangs, a ponytail, and a friendly smile. First Dora showed her all the animals. Then they came in and sat on the settee, and Dora asked in a small voice, "Mam, what could we do?"

"It's such a lovely Indian summer day, how about going for a boat ride," I suggested.

"Yes, let's!" Dora cried eagerly, jumping up. "I'll get the oars."

As she passed me in the kitchen, she whispered, "Cheryl

didn't like the animals, and she was afraid of the cows."

We all trudged down to the boat, and the children clambered happily aboard, all except Cheryl. "I don't think I want to go boating," she protested in a strained voice.

"C'mon," Dora urged. "Hop in. It's really fun. Please."

But Cheryl shook her head and refused to get in the boat.

"Are you afraid?" Dora asked bluntly.

"No!" Cheryl's lips trembled, and tears squeezed under her eyelids.

"All right, let's go in and make some cookies," I suggested. But then Crist began to cry.

"I want to go for a boat ride; I want to, I want to," he cried, his voice rising. Cheryl covered her ears with her hands. "Wow! That kid can yell."

Back in the kitchen, the youngsters all pulled up chairs around the table to help mix the cookie dough. I gave them cookie cutters, and that kept them happy and occupied until suppertime.

At the supper table, when the mush and milk were passed, Cheryl held it at arm's length to pass it and exclaimed, "Yuck!" She did take a small helping of mashed potatoes and beef, but the succotash she eyed with contempt, same as the mush.

After supper Dora washed the dishes, and Cheryl dried them. She whispered to Dora, though, that she never had to dry dishes at home. "We have an electric dishwasher," she bragged condescendingly.

Dora took it as an insult. "So what," she countered. "We have something you don't have. We have a spring in the cellar."

"A what?"

"A spring in the cellar. Come, and I'll show it to you."
They skipped down the broad stone steps to the damp cellar, and Dora showed her the spring. I stood at the top of the steps and listened to their conversation. Cheryl seemed impressed, and I believe Dora felt vindicated.

"Where does the water come from?" Cheryl wondered. "Is it good to drink?"

"It comes out of the ground and flows back under the ground. It keeps our milk cold, and in the summertime we put watermelons in to make them cold, or drinks like iced tea. But we don't drink the water."

"That's neat! It's almost as good as a refrigerator."

"We do have a gas refrigerator upstairs in the washhouse, though," Dora informed her. "There's a little freezer compartment in it where we keep ice cream sometimes."

"What's in that big bin over in the corner?" Cheryl asked, pointing to the potato bin.

Dora mischievously replied, "That's where bad girls and boys get locked in when they disobey."

Cheryl screamed and dashed up the steps.

"Dora!" I called sharply. "You stop teasing Cheryl. She won't want to come again if you frighten her like that."

"Where's your TV set?" Cheryl wanted to know.

Dora gave her a strange look. "We don't have a TV. Didn't you know that?"

"No TV?" There was a look of disbelief on Cheryl's face. "But I watch TV every evening until bedtime."

"We can play with my Cabbage Patch doll," Dora offered, running upstairs to get her.

"But I don't want to play with your doll. I want to watch TV," wailed Cheryl.

Dora came down with the doll and showed her to Cheryl. "Here, take her!"

Cheryl half-heartedly took the doll, stared at her for a moment, then griped in a horrified voice, "This doll doesn't have a face!" She threw the doll into a corner with such force that her bonnet flew off. Then she flopped face-down on the settee. "This is weird, disgusting. It's absolutely gross!"

Just then Nate came in and heard the last sentence. "What's wrong?" He asked quizzically, with raised eyebrows.

Cheryl suddenly jumped up. "May I use your telephone? I think I'll call my mom and ask her to take me home. I'm ready to go home now."

"But you wanted to sleep with me in my bed," Dora protested. "Don't go now. Besides, we don't have a telephone."

"Rats!" Cheryl stamped her foot. "No TV, no dishwasher, no telephone, no faces on the dolls!"

"Would you like to cut out some paper dolls and their clothes?" I asked, hoping to get her interested in something. "Or maybe color a picture in Dora's new coloring book?"

Cheryl shook her head disdainfully. "That's kid stuff. I'm not a baby anymore."

Nate suggested a game of musical chairs. He got down his Marine Band harmonica from the clock shelf and explained the rules of the game to the children. Nate would play the harmonica while they marched in a circle. When he stopped playing, they must all scramble for a chair. There was one less chair than players, and whoever didn't make it to a chair had to stand in the center next time.

They all loved this, even Cheryl, and they played, breathless and panting, until it was time for devotions. After that, I went upstairs with them to tuck everyone in.

"Better get the comforters out," Nate told me. "It feels like Indian summer is over. There's a cold northwest wind blowing up, and the temperature is dropping."

I heard the wheel of the windmill whining and clanging. Cheryl asked fearfully, "What's that awful noise?"

Dora laughed, "That's just the wind wheel. You aren't afraid of a wind wheel, are you?"

"I don't like the sound of it," Cheryl complained in a small voice.

After tucking them in, a little *Englische* and a little Amish side by side, I tiptoed downstairs and hoped they would sleep. It was a windy night, the house was creaking, and the wind wheel whining. I remembered how it had disturbed me when Nate was in Ohio. Would Cheryl be frightened?

I had just fallen into a deep sleep when I heard a small voice calling, "Mam, mam, wake up! Cheryl's crying and she wants to go home."

I struck a match and lit the kerosene lamp. The alarm clock showed 10:00 p.m. I hurriedly dressed and found the crying Cheryl in the kitchen. Dora had her arm around her, trying to comfort her.

"I want to go home," sobbed Cheryl. "Please take me home right now."

I tried a dozen different suggestions to persuade her it would be all right to wait until morning. But Cheryl turned down everything and cried more hysterically.

"I want my mommy! Take me home now!" she wailed.

Finally I woke Nate and told him the story.

"Couldn't we just spank her and make her go to bed?" he suggested irritably.

"It wouldn't work," I replied. "She's already getting hysterical. What shall we do with her?"

He groaned and rolled over. "I worked hard all day, and I have to be up early tomorrow morning. It sure *ferlates* (disgusts) me to go hitch up the horse and take her home."

"I suppose I could walk out to the phone shanty and call her mother," I volunteered. "She could come and pick Cheryl up."

Nate gladly accepted my offer and went back to sleep. The girls agreed to sit on the settee until I returned.

The moon was bright and the wind crisp as I hurried out the lane, flashlight in hand. At the end of the lane I came face to face with a skunk. We both turned, but the skunk was quicker. There was a powerful stench, and I couldn't get away from it. I started to run, but my eyes watered, tears ran down over my cheeks, and I stumbled.

Finally I reached the washhouse door and quickly got rid of my clothes, tossing them on a heap in the grass. First I washed myself with tomato juice, then I filled the big washtub with water, got a washcloth and a bar of homemade soap, and scrubbed for all I was worth.

As I tiptoed shivering through the kitchen, wrapped in a towel, the lamp on the table shed a glow over the Amish-*englisch* pair fast asleep on the settee. I covered them with a blanket and sneaked off to bed. "One more whimper out of you," I murmured, "and I'll take Nate's advice."

Thankfully, when I woke again, it was to the sound of excited giggles coming from two little girls setting the breakfast table to surprise me. 🦌

*F*ew positions in life are so full of importunities as that of the mother of a family and mistress of a house. She may have a dozen interruptions while writing one letter or settling an account. What holiness, what self-control is needed to be always calm and unruffled amid these little vexations, never manifesting the slightest impatience!

Pausing in work without apparent annoyance, replying with a smile on the lips, waiting patiently the end of a long conversation, and finally returning calmly to the yet unfinished task—all this is the sign of a recollected soul, one that waits upon God. Oh! What blessings are shed around them by such patient souls . . . but alas! how rarely we meet with them.

I'm feeling comforted to hear that such souls are rare (misery loves company). I had a hectic Monday and sadly felt lacking in patience. Nate left early for the last week of corn-picking on the Foster farm.

I collected all the laundry and sorted it. I wanted to get an early start, for the days are getting shorter, and it's harder to get the wash dry by evening. All went well for the first two loads. Then while I was hanging up the wash, Peter wanted to help me, and he tried to put a load through. He thoroughly jammed the wringer, and it stalled the engine.

I angrily turned to Peter. "Why did you do it? Now the wringer's stuck. Your hand might have caught in it!"

Peter crept away with tears in his eyes. I unraveled the dress from the wringer and yanked on the starter cord to start the engine. Nothing happened. Again and again I yanked it until I was thoroughly exhausted.

"If only Nate or Rudy were here," I moaned. "Maybe it needs a new spark plug."

I rested awhile, then yanked some more, and finally it roared to life, smoking and shaking. But I soon discovered that the wringer was broken beyond my ability to fix it. So I had to twist out by hand the rest of the wash, like the pioneer women did.

After the third load, I heard the children calling me in alarm, "Mam, come quick! The horses are out!"

Oh no! I dashed to the door, and there in the lane ran four horses, heads held high, tails flying in the wind. Following behind was Nellie's colt. What if they ran out on the road and were hit by a truck? Could I chase them in alone? I decided to try.

If only I could sneak around them and head them off before they trotted out the lane. I sidled slowly past them, and just when I thought I'd accomplished it, Nellie's head went up, and she snorted and dashed out the lane, followed by the other horses. My heart sank.

A car was coming, and the driver slammed on the brakes with a screeching of tires. Pamela Styer got out. "I'll help," she called. "I'll try not to let them get past me and head them back in the lane."

The barnyard gate was open, and Pamela courageously approached the horses, waving her arms. They turned and trotted in the lane, I directed them toward the gate, and obediently they galloped in. I heaved a sigh of relief and called my thanks to Pamela. She waved and drove off.

But my troubles weren't over yet. I heard a bawling inside the barn and found a freshening cow (giving birth), and it looked like she might need help. I decided to check on her later, after I quickly finished hanging out the wash.

Then I heard Crist crying at the top of his lungs in the kitchen. He had pulled down and spilled all over himself my bowl of sour dough starter for bread making. His hair, face, shirt, and pants were dripping with it. I sat down hard. I thought I was going to bawl, but when I saw how comical Crist looked, I began to laugh instead, albeit rather shakily.

"*So gehts eens gute geh* (so goes one's good going)," I told myself. How trifling these little annoyances would seem in the face of a real tragedy.

When I had scrubbed up Crist, finished the wash, gone to the phone shanty and called the vet, and prepared us some lunch, I told the children they could each pick out a book and I would read it to them (translating it into Dutch as I go). I wanted to make it up to them for being uptight and short with them, and they freely forgave me. Precious little souls.

Oh God, I thank you for them, our dearest treasures. Help me to lead them in the paths of righteousness, for your sake and theirs. ❧

November 24, Thanksgiving Day

*R*udy and Barbianne's wedding day. I suppose if the old saying holds true, they'll get rich, for it snowed all day. I don't know whether it means rich in money, or rich in love; hopefully both. The roads were in good condition for sleighing, so Nate hitched the horse to the bobsled, and we all happily piled in.

We were in a singing mood, and first we sang,

Over the river and through the woods,
     to Barbianne's house we go.
The horse knows the way to carry the sleigh,
     through the white and drifted snow. . . .
                              —Lydia Marie Child

Then Nate started the hymn,

     Come, heaven bound pilgrims,
          and join in God's praise,
     Come seek now his blessing
          and learn of his ways,
     In humble devotion
          bow low at his feet,
     In true spirit worship,
          His favor entreat.
                              —J. M. Shenk

We were soon in a string of up-headed and prancing horses hitched to sleighs and buggies, driving in the lane at the Fisher home, where the wedding was held. Our assignment was to help prepare the roast. When we entered the washhouse, good smells were already coming from the kitchen. The house was spotless, and the big folding doors were opened to make one big room, with backless benches set in neat rows for the guests.

Barbianne and Rudy made a fine couple. Her cheeks were rosy and her eyes shone, and he looked handsome and manly in his new suit.

The wedding sermon was an inspiration, not just to the wedding couple but to all the listeners, to strive for harmonious Christian living, to show kind affection to each other, and in honor to prefer one another. The preacher called for husbands to love their wives as Christ loved the church and gave himself for it, and for wives to be chaste, discreet, keepers at home, subject to their husbands, and to love and reverence them.

Just as we arose from kneeling for the last prayer, there was a terrific crash, and clanging and splashing. I caught a glimpse of Barbianne's mother's face, and there was such a look of consternation and despair on it! I didn't blame her a bit, for it caused quite a commotion until everything was cleaned up. A small wooden table had collapsed under the weight of a kettle of water.

The bridal party was seated at the beautiful *Eck* (corner) table, and the wedding cake was absolutely gorgeous. The meal was delicious (even the roast) and the *gschtammde Grummbiere* (mashed potatoes) were smooth and fluffy.

When the last dish had been washed, we spent the rest of the afternoon singing hymns and visiting. I'm glad to see Barbianne and Rudy happily married and starting a home of their own. We wish them God's blessings and many happy years together. 🙦

A Blessed Christmas Recipe

Take the crisp cold air of a December night, add two generous parts of snow. Into a generous heart, stir air so clear it tingles. Mix the wonders of a little girl, the sparkle of a little boy's glance, the love of parents, the sweetness of the grace of God. Set beside the chimney. Let the mixture rise in the dream of goodwill toward men.

It will be ready to bake when it bubbles with warmth and good feeling. Bake in an oven of kindness and love, Bedeck with the twinkling of a bright star in the east. Serve to the tune of the ancient Christmas carol, sung by all the family.

This recipe is sufficient for young and old, all whom you meet through the holiday season (unknown, adapted).

The memories of Amanda have been growing fainter, but this Christmas season has brought them back sharply. So it's a time of both sorrow and rejoicing, sorrow that she is no longer with us, and rejoicing that she is with Jesus, and that we will see her again someday.

Nate read the children Christmas stories from the Bible, about Mary, Joseph, and Baby Jesus, the star in the east, and the heavenly host announcing, "Peace on earth, good will toward men."

Then with great excitement, they opened their packages. Dora received the skates she had planned on for a long time already, and Peter got a little homemade wheel-barrow—("just like Dad's," he proudly claimed, his ruddy face glowing with happiness).

For Sadie, Nate had made a little wooden doll bed, and I made a dolly patchwork quilt for it. She came and threw her arms around me, lisping, "*Denki, Mam* (thanks, Mom)," her dark eyes shining. And for Crist-ly, as I some-times call him, there was a homemade riding horse. He galloped through the house with it, whinnying like a colt. As I often ponder these things, I think, What have I done to deserve such beautiful lovable children?

Nate bundled them up and took them outside to go sledding while I prepared Christmas dinner for Grandpa Daves, and Henry, Priscilla, and Miriam. I roasted a young turkey stuffed with bread dressing, also mashed potatoes, sweet potatoes, peas, cranberry relish. . . . For dessert, I prepared whoopie pies, chocolate shoofly pies, fruit salad, and an ice-cream custard—ready for freezing in the after-noon.

I felt almost guilty making such a feast when I know there are hungry, starving children in other lands who would be glad for even a cup of plain, cooked rice. We do give through the Christian aid ministries, but are we giving enough?

Priscilla was laughing gaily (almost giddily so). Henry also seemed more like himself again, and Miriam was pret-tier than ever.

Grandpa Dave was in one of his storytelling moods, and he kept us all entertained. At 3:00 o'clock there was a knock on the door. There were Gloria and George, loaded down with brightly wrapped packages, which they distrib-uted to us.

Nate fetched a sackful of ice from the creek, smashed it with the sledgehammer, and got down our hand-crank ice cream freezer. I filled the tank with custard and cream, and the tub with ice and rock salt. The men took turns cranking it. When it started to crank too hard, Nate lifted the lid, took out the dasher, and scooped out dishfuls of vanilla ice cream for everyone.

George commented that he'd never tasted homemade ice cream, and Henry told him he'd missed half his life. He loves the stuff, especially topped with chocolate sauce and eaten with pretzels. Henry informed George, "If you want good, old-fashioned, sumptuous country cooking with down-home taste, try Amish cooking. It can't be beat."

I've been thinking about what he said, especially the word *sumptuous*. I know we Amish are noted for our good cooking, but do we fare sumptuously every day, like it says in the Bible, in Jesus' account of the rich man? I hope not. We should be satisfied with simple, common, homegrown foods.

I often think of Allen and Frieda's Grandma, and her theories of eating foods only in the way God gave them to us. Maybe we would do well to follow her advice more.

Tonight we had Christmas carolers, Amish youth, who left a fruit basket at our door. Thank-you, God, for kind friends. ❧

Amish or Not

A brand-new year, and I've made my list of resolutions:

1. I will not raise my voice (or yell) at the children. It loses its effect, and it should not be necessary. A spanking is better, if a command in a quiet tone of voice is not obeyed.

2. I will make every day a hunting trip to see good in my children. I will find something for which to sincerely praise them (not mere flattery).

3. I will show appreciation to my husband and never take for granted what he does for me, how hard he works to provide for his family.

4. I will never grumble or complain about anything, and I will try not to show impatience.

Nate found my list on the bedroom bureau and read it (I wondered what he was chuckling about). "So you do appreciate me. I thought maybe you hadn't gotten over wishing you'd married Allen yet."

I threw the rocking chair cushion at him, and he ducked and bumped his head on the bedpost. It served him right. 🐿

Dora's friendship with Cheryl seems to be the lasting kind. On Monday Dora came home from school all smiles, saying she was invited to Cheryl's place for the night again, on Tuesday.

"I can hardly wait! We're having pizza and milkshakes again. And we'll watch TV."

"I don't think you'll be allowed to go this time," I told her, quietly but firmly. "Dad and I have decided that once was enough."

"No!" she shouted, stamping her foot, her eyes flashing.

In that moment I thought she looked just like Priscilla once had when she stamped her foot at me.

"Dora," I used the most authoritative voice I could muster. "Go upstairs to your room right now. You will not talk back like that to me."

She went, but the rebellious look was still on her face. When Nate came in, he went upstairs, disciplined her, and again told her she could not go to Cheryl's house, and that TV was a bad influence on children with its violence and wickedness.

When Dora came downstairs, I was not entirely happy with the look on her face (was it a determined look?). But she was quiet and obeyed without hesitation, doing her work, and even doing some things without being told.

After the dishes were finished, I got out the lace and glue, red construction paper and stickers, and we sat down to make valentines. I thought it might be a pleasant diversion for Dora, and she helped willingly enough, but said little. Peter pasted and colored busily (with his tongue in his cheek), Sadie cut out hearts with her blunt little scissors, and even Cristly helped.

When Nate was finished with the chores, he came in. He wanted to be extra kind because he thought Dora was probably feeling bad about not being allowed to go home with Cheryl, so he told the children interesting stories until bedtime. When they knelt to say their bedtime prayers, Dora refused to say hers. We decided to let it go, hoping she would soon be feeling better.

Then on Wednesday when it was time for Dora to come home, I saw the school bus driving right past without stopping, and I knew that could mean only one thing—Dora had disobeyed and gotten off the school bus at Cheryl's house.

I told Nate about it. He hitched up the horse right away and drove to Cheryl's and brought her back. She was crying when they drove in the lane forty-five minutes later, a small forlorn figure, curled on the buggy seat beside Nate, rubbing her eyes with her fists. I felt a stab of sympathy for her. But that changed when she came over to where I was washing outside windows and announced, "I'm _____ mad!"

"Dora!" I cried, shocked. "Where did you learn such language?"

"I learned it from Cheryl," she reported defiantly. "I'm so mad that Dad made me come home. I wasn't going to watch TV, honest I wasn't."

"But you still disobeyed by going," I reminded her, "and all disobedience must be punished."

Dora stamped her foot. "I'm not your daughter!" she declared angrily, then rushed into the house.

My heart sank and I felt weak all over. "Oh, God," I cried, "what did we do wrong? What shall we do? If Dora is this rebellious at six, what will she be like at sixteen?" Tears coursed down my cheeks as I went to find Nate.

"I guess Grandpa Dave was right," Nate commented sadly when I told him. "He said we'd be sorry if we sent Dora to public school."

I nodded soberly and said, "Now we'll have to think of a suitable punishment."

"I think she should be spanked," Nate decided, "and have some of her privileges taken away, until she shows signs of being sorry and of showing submission. She's headstrong, and if we don't get it out of her now, what will she be like when she's a teenager?"

As I turned to go into the house, I saw a big gray and silver van driving in the lane. Through the window I saw unfamiliar faces framed by black bonnets and broad-rimmed hats. Plain people! Who could it be? Nate was smiling broadly, and I could tell that he knew them well.

"So here come the Yoder brothers!" he exclaimed amiably. "It's good to see you all!"

We all shook hands, and I greeted their wives with a holy kiss. The Yoders had lived as neighbors to Nate over thirty-five years ago. They had gone to school with him until their family had moved to Indiana.

"You're welcome to stay for supper," Nate invited them.

"Well, we just might do that if you don't go to any trouble," agreed Gideon, the oldest.

"Tomato soup is fine," one of the women put in. "Everyday fare is good enough for us."

I took them into the house, and they helped peel potatoes, set the table, and slice the dried beef. I knew that even though they had said tomato soup would be fine, they would think me a poor hostess if I served that instead of a full-course meal.

Dora came downstairs and helped, and she was docile and submissive enough to suit anyone.

The men went to the barn with Nate to do chores together. After supper they sat and talked about their school days.

"Remember the time you talked back to the teacher and had to stand in the corner?" Benuel asked Nate.

Nate blushed, so I knew it was true. I was all ears. I could hardly believe it. Thankfully, the children were already in bed.

"How about the time you sailed a paper jet up to the teacher's desk, and he marched you up front, pulling your ears all the way?" Nate shot back.

Now it was Benuel's turn to blush.

"He wasn't as mad that time as he was when Eli snapped a corn kernel up front with his suspenders. Poor Eli lost some of his hair."

Eli's face got red, and he soberly confided, "From that day on, I began to get bald, and now my hair's nearly gone."

107

His droll way of speaking made everyone laugh.

One of the wives commented, "You aren't being very nice to each other. Surely there are some good things to tell."

There was much teasing, laughter, and storytelling. Then at 10:00 p.m. the van driver returned, and they left for their night lodgings.

"So you were naughty, too, sometimes," I kidded Nate, as we prepared for bed.

He grinned. "Those three were a bad influence on me. Their first, middle, and last names were mischief, and they pulled me into it, too."

Suddenly I remembered Dora. We had forgotten all about her when the company came, and now the thought of it lay like a dreadful pall on my heart.

"Listen!" exclaimed Nate. "What's that sound I hear?"

We opened the bedroom door softly, and there it was again—a tiny sob. We tiptoed down the hall to Dora's room. She was crying softly.

"What's wrong?" Nate asked.

"I—I can't sleep, and my belly hurts," she sobbed. "I—I'm sorry I disobeyed and talked back and said those bad words." She buried her face in her pillow, and her sobs were muffled by it.

"Have you asked Jesus to forgive you?" Nate gently wondered. Dora shook her head.

"Why don't you do it now?" I suggested. "And ask him to help you to be obedient and submissive after this."

Dora slipped out of bed and knelt beside it. We helped her pray and talked to her awhile longer. Then she went happily to bed, feeling much better because she'd confessed her wrongs and made things right. 🍂

*T*hank You, God
Life can hold such lovely things
Apple blossom scented springs;
Purple mist of haze and heather;
Books to read in stormy weather.
Common as a cookie jar,
Things I hold the dearest are:
A small white house, a small brown dog;
Sunlight breaking through a fog;
And as sweet as summer rain,
Understanding after pain.
Life holds all these lovely things.
Thank-you, God, for all it brings.
—Nina Stiles

I'm trying to count my blessings tonight, trying to concentrate on "life's lovely things" and not to dwell on my problems.

My baby is three years old today! He's still small for his age, but wiry and quick, bright-eyed and alert as ever. He loves horses and puppies and being outside with Nate. Yet when he comes in tired, he goes right to the bookcase for his favorite book. His day wouldn't be complete without it. He still likes my lap, to be rocked and cuddled.

Dora begged to be allowed to make him a birthday cake. She even iced it and decorated it with raisins, and she sang a solo of "Happy Birthday" for him.

Cristly loves when Miriam comes to play. He leads her around and watches out for her, as her protector and friend.

Lately Miriam has often been here because Priscilla is holding Tupperware parties. Even when she isn't having a party, others have told us that sometimes a car is parked in their drive all evening. We don't know who is there or what they're up to, for Priscilla and Henry don't want to talk about the matter. Whenever I think about it, I feel heavyhearted.

This evening I saw a robin hopping about, which cheered me considerably. To me, a robin sweetly singing is a messenger of God's love and goodness and mercy. ❧

March 28

*M*oving day for Barbianne and Rudy, to the Foster farm. A fine spring rain was falling, with robins singing everywhere. The peas are up in the garden, also onions and radishes. It always makes me rejoice to see the neat rows of little greens peeping through.

We helped them unpack and get settled, carrying in boxes and boxes of dishes, bedding, shiny new pots and pans and towels. The men lugged in the nice new furniture. By tonight everything was in place.

I like that kitchen, its big triple window facing the barn, the wide windowsill for houseplants, a built-in corner cupboard with glass doors, and woodwork and wainscoting regrained just a few years ago. The settee and the combination hutch and china closet were both made by Rudy's dad, and they match perfectly.

Barbianne hung up a wooden motto that she had received as a wedding gift, with this prayer on it:

Bless Our Marriage

We thank you, God, for the love you have implanted in our hearts. May it always inspire us to be kind in our words, considerate of feelings, and concerned for each other's needs and wishes. Help us to be understanding and forgiving of human weaknesses and failings. Increase our faith and trust in you, and may your prudence guide our life and love. Bless our marriage, oh God, with peace and happiness, and make our love fruitful for your glory and our joy, both here and in eternity. Amen.

Barbianne and Rudy are glowing with love and happiness now—just as Priscilla and Henry were a few short years ago but don't seem to be anymore. I believe they still love each other, but no longer do they have the peace of submission, a yielded will, and a quiet conscience. I pray for God to give them wisdom and understanding to make the decision that leads to the way of righteousness. ❧

April 21

I could hardly believe my eyes this morning—snow so late in the season! But it was true, still snowing, and even drifting a bit.

Nate came in from choring and said a heifer fell and broke her leg, and we're going to have to butcher her right away. He drove to Grandpa Dave's place for the butchering equipment, then drove over to pick up Priscilla and bring her along to help.

When she walked in the door, I stifled a gasp. Over her usual Amish dress, she wore a blue-flowered apron! Surely she knew that plain material without stripes, designs, or prints is required in our *Ordnung*. What next?

Pamela Styer came for milk, and when she heard that we're having butchering day, she asked if she could stay and watch. She and Priscilla hit it off well, and by noon they sounded like old friends.

Pamela helped to grind the meat, cook the pudding (leftover meat scraps), and stuff the casings for sausage and bologna. At 4:00 o'clock she offered to drive Priscilla home.

They went out the door, laughing and chattering gaily. Pamela pronounced it a most interesting day and that she had gathered a lot of material for her novel. ❧

May 12

*T*he meadow is filled with buttercups and lush green grass, the meadowlarks are singing, and the fit-fit-fit-fit of the flicker can be heard most anytime. Apple and pear trees are blossoming, and I think of a verse of a poem I learned in school:

> How much more beautiful are trees
>   When blossoms come from them in May!
> How much more beautiful are you
>   When loving words are all you say!
>   —*Molly Rodman*

The Amish schools are out for summer vacation, but Dora still has to go until the second week of June. A few weeks ago we visited her school, and Dora was not happy to see us. She didn't smile once. Instead, there was a slight frown on her face, and she hardly ever glanced our way.

When she came home after school, she asked, "Mam, why did you come? Why did you wear your bonnet and shawl?"

Then I realized that she, poor child, was ashamed of us. She's the only plain girl in her class. Oh, well, it will be different next year when she goes to our own Amish school. ❦

June 18

*R*ain is raining all around
   It falls on farm and field.
It is a satisfying sound
   And insures a bounteous yield.

—Unknown

Heavy rains and flooding have been our portion this week, and the creek is high. I'm careful to keep the children inside when it's a rushing, raging river like that, after our experience with Dora a few years ago, but I like to look at it myself. There's something exhilarating yet humbling and awesome about mighty floodwaters.

Last evening we had a heavy thunderstorm. Lightning struck a big sycamore tree in the meadow and split it in two.

We were thankful that the horses and cows were safe in the barn, for if they'd have been standing under that tree, as they often do, they no doubt would've been killed.

The garden is a sea of mud, and the strawberries are rotting on the vines. Dora did find enough, though, to make a strawberry shortcake for my birthday. She said she's going to have a birthday party for me, and that she has invited company for supper as a surprise for me. She wanted to make the meal by herself and told me to sit in the parlor until it's ready.

I sat and wondered and waited, working on a bit of embroidery to pass the time. At 6:00 o'clock, a tearful Dora came to the parlor door with word that the company didn't show up. She had invited only Cheryl. Yesterday, all by herself, she had gone to the phone shanty to call her! Perhaps there was some misunderstanding.

I consoled her the best I could and told her that Cheryl had no way of letting us know that she couldn't come after all. We then had a jolly meal of chocolate milk, sandwiches, and strawberry shortcake. They all pulled my ears until they were sore.

Peter is just learning to count, and he thought that as far as he had to count, I must be pretty near a hundred years old! Dear, funny family! Thank you, heavenly Father for them all! ❧

July 25

*Y*esterday morning when we got up and went to the barn to do the chores, a shaggy, unkempt-looking horse, hitched to a dilapidated old cart, was tied to the ring under the forebay. We wondered what was going on. And then we heard a man's voice, singing inside the barn.

There's a train that's bound for glory,
  And there is no other way.
    If you want to go, If you want to go.
  Get your ticket ready, for this train may come today,
    If you want to go, If you want to go.
  We are going to glory, we are happy all the way.
    All is glory and rejoicing every day.
  Jesus is our great conductor,
    He has been this way before,
      If you want to go, If you want to go.
                                    —*Unknown*

"Who in the world could that be?" Nate muttered. The barn door opened and a seedy-looking man emerged, wearing a floppy black broad-rimmed Amish hat, a flowing beard, and baggy broadfall pants held up by wide suspenders.

"Howdy folks!" he called, revealing a toothless grin. "Would you have a bite of breakfast for an old feller like me, and a bit of grain for my horse?"

"Who are you?" Nate asked with narrowed eyes.

The man lifted a hand. "Now, now, don't get riled. I'm just a harmless old man. I'd like to join the Amish, that is, if you'll have me. I traveled all the way up from Oley Valley with this horse, stopping at farms along the way. My name is Oscar Thompson, and as I said, I'd like to join your Amish church."

"Well, all right, you can stay for breakfast," Nate told him. "You can unhitch if you want to."

"Thank you, thank you, may the good Lord bless!" Oscar beamed his gratitude and again began singing at the top of his lungs.

"What an odd, funny old character," I observed to Nate, when we were alone. "Do you think he is to be trusted?"

"He says he's harmless," Nate chuckled, "and he acts like he's not all there. But maybe that's just a ruse. Keep the children away from him until we learn more about him."

Oscar spent the day doing odd jobs, then asked to sleep in the barn. This morning when we got up, he was gone. I heaved a sigh of relief, for it was rather hard to keep the children away from him. He has his pockets full of candy and likes to talk with them and tease them.

This afternoon we were at the grocery store and met Emanuel Yoder. He said Oscar already spent a day each with some of the other farms around here, and even asked for the bishop's name and where he lives so he can go to see him about joining church. He likes to attend horse sales and also plans to attend our next church service.

Emanuel seems to think he's nothing but a tramp who wants to live off the Amish for awhile. I guess time will tell what he really is after. ❧

August 29

A cooling breeze is stirring the curtains, and oh, it sure feels good to relax in my own bed. Was it only on Monday morning that I awoke with bad pain? I shook Nate awake and was whimpering like a puppy. I just couldn't help it.

"What's wrong?" He was suddenly alert and alarmed.

"I—I have an unbearable pain in my abdomen," I gasped. "On the right side." I was enveloped by another sharp spasm of pain, and an involuntary moan escaped my lips.

Quickly he lighted the lamp, dressed, and came over to my side of the bed. His face was a mixture of concern and pity.

"Shall I call the doctor?" He was looking almost like a frightened little boy.

"Yes, or rather, go to Pamela Styer and ask her if she can take me to the emergency room at the hospital. It feels like my appendix is bursting." I groaned as a fresh attack seized me. "Hurry! I can't stand this much longer."

Nate hurried, but it still seemed like ages before I heard the purr of a motor in the lane. It was Pamela, and Nate was with her, along with Henry, Priscilla, and Miriam, too. They all looked like angels to me.

"Henry's going to do the milking before he leaves for work, and Priscilla will stay with the children," Nate told me. "Let's go."

The trip to the hospital, even with Pamela's expert and careful driving, was a nightmare. I was relieved to be ushered into the care of the white-coated doctors and nurses. The thought went through my mind that the time to serve the Lord is when one is well. When the mind is fogged with pain, praying is nothing but a frantic plea for help.

A short time later they operated on me, and thankfully, the appendix had not burst; it was only perforated. There was some leakage, and I had to stay at the hospital a day longer because of it. After I didn't feel quite so sick anymore, I began to miss my family. I had all kinds of thoughts, probably because of my weakened condition.

What if a rabid fox should bite Sadie again? What if Oscar Thompson came back and kidnapped Dora? What if

Peter ran away, like he once threatened to do, and took Crist with him, and we'd never see them again? Such thoughts made me feel weak and trembly. I realized that it was my nerves, and that I'd have to quit letting my imagination run away with me.

Nate's visits were like a ray of sunshine in my days, and he reassured me that all was fine at home. I began to feel better every day. Today I came home just before lunch and

found Abner K.'s Mary (daughter of Abner K.) here doing the work and caring for the children. She's friendly and cheerful and can stay for two weeks.

The house was spick-and-span, my bed freshly made, and a bouquet of lovely gladiolus on the bureau. "Be it ever so humble, there's no place like home!" (Payne). The children all crowded around my bed, and they looked incredibly dear and precious. Yet I was so conscious of the little face that was missing—the one that is with Jesus, beholding his glory, and like unto the angels. ❧

September 3

*T*he new schoolhouse is finished, and just in time. When we told Dora she wouldn't be going to the same school this year, she cried for her friend Cheryl. But this morning she walked to school happily enough.

Grandpa Daves gave a piece of their land to build the schoolhouse on, and this summer the men and women of this district have been helping all they can. After the foundation was in, the men gathered one day to raise the building and close it in. This was followed by plastering, painting, varnishing, and then cleaning up.

Rosemary's sister Ruth is the teacher. I could hardly believe our good fortune when I heard that, for if she's anything like her sister, she'll be good.

I'm thankful that Dora doesn't have far to walk to school, and that those thieves in the trailer are gone; Pamela is there instead. She came over yesterday and breezed cheerily in the door, bringing me an ABC sunshine box: twenty-six small packages marked from *A* to *Z*, and I'm only allowed to open one a day, starting with *A*, and so on. If all the *englisch* people were like her. . . .

Yesterday's *A* package contained a big shiny red apple and a tin can of asparagus. Today's *B* package contained a beautiful bookmark and a little handwoven basket. I wonder what tomorrow's *C* package will be. Candy?

I'm also getting get-well cards from friends and relatives every day. On Monday evening Henry and Priscilla brought supper over for the whole family, and last night Grandpa Daves brought the meal. Whatever would we do without kind friends?

Mary K. (as we call her) is a good worker, and the children love her. She canned twenty-five quarts of peaches today.

Happiness is—feeling well, being able to eat again, and enjoying it.

Bringing in a beautiful bouquet of marigolds and zinnias.

Seeing Nate with the children gathered around him, telling them a Bible story.

Hearing the ping of lids sealing on the peach cans.

Getting a letter from Rosemary and Isaac.

Walking down to the creek with the children, and seeing the beauties of nature.

Trusting in God's love and his goodness, whate'er betide.

A joyous heart. . . . ❧

*D*ora comes skipping home from school each evening, happy and contented.

"I like this school so much better," she told me tonight. "I have lots of friends, and teacher Ruth is my friend, too."

I remembered how she had cried when she couldn't go back to public school. Isn't that the way it often is? We pray earnestly for something and cry when the prayer isn't answered the way we'd like it to be. Later we thank God that it wasn't, for he has given us something much better.

Already Dora's been given a Bible verse to memorize: "O taste and see that the Lord is good: blessed is the one who trusts in him." Now I hear her singing hymns instead of those silly, meaningless secular songs they sang in music class at the public school. And there's no one asking her to go along home to watch TV. Are we thankful enough for the privilege of having our own schools?

I am feeling better every day, getting my strength back gradually, and feeling immensely grateful. Why do we have to lose our health before we can fully appreciate it? ❧

I received a big package in the mail today, and I believe I was as excited as the children. They crowded around me, shoving and elbowing each other, wanting to get as close as possible. Finally the last of the tape and wrapping was torn off, and there was a lovely homemade scrapbook from little Mary, Allen and Polly's daughter.

It brought memories crowding back of when I was working for widower Allen, and Mary was just three years old—blond, blue-eyed, and everyone's darling. Now she must already be in third or fourth grade. How time flies!

She had a letter included, too, saying that all the pupils in their school each made a scrapsheet for me in art classes, and they put them together in a book. She wrote about how cute her little brother Daniel is and that her older sister Rachel now has a beau, Simon Peachy.

I must send a letter and a thank you card right away. The children and I spent a lot of time looking at the scrapbook—it's a priceless volume containing pictures, Bible verses, poems, and words of cheer and encouragement.

Thank you, Father, for your wondrous blessings of kind friends and loved ones, and help me to pass on to others the kindness bestowed on me.

October 8

*T*hy kingdom come,
    with power and grace,
To every heart of man;
Thy peace and joy and righteousness
    In all our bosoms reign.

—*Charles Wesley*

Peace, joy, and righteousness, a Christian can have, but there is no such thing as perfect happiness on this earth. That will have to wait for heaven, when all sin will be destroyed and all tears wiped away.

Henry and Priscilla have been a constant source of

heartache to us since they've begun to flounder in the faith. They attend church services occasionally, not regularly. Lately I've seen Priscilla driving by with Pamela a lot, sometimes several times a week. She goes without her bonnet, and Miriam still looks like a little *englisch* girl.

It will soon be time for communion services again, and Henry and Priscilla have already missed it twice, if again they deliberately don't partake of communion this time, they will likely be excommunicated and put in the ban. If only they would be willing to confide in someone.

Did Henry lead Priscilla astray, or was it the other way around? For October 11, *Faschtdaag* (fast day), I've decided to spend the whole day fasting and praying for them. Prayer changes things. I told Nate about it, and he promised to do the same.

Dear, kindhearted Nate. ❧

November 9

*I*t's so good to feel completely recovered, to have my strength back again. I thank God daily for it.

Now I am more aware of the sweetness and loveliness of life and the preciousness of good health. The world has a newness, almost as if I'd be really seeing it for the first time—things such as an exhilarating wind before a storm comes up, wild geese winging their way overhead, the sheen of golden leaves floating down, and the sweet, tangy taste of freshly pressed cider.

I spent the day happily raking leaves. It was a mild autumn day of ripe sunshine and pungent earth smells. The children "helped" by gleefully jumping into the piles and scattering them.

Midafternoon, a by-now-familiar, tired-looking horse and a dilapidated old cart came trundling in the lane, accompanied by the sound of carefree singing.

"Oscar! Oscar!" Peter shouted. "Candy!"

He was off like a flash to meet Oscar at the barn. Sighing, I followed him. I didn't want Peter to be out there alone.

"Howdy, missus," Oscar called, raising his hand. "Would you have a bite of supper for a harmless old man tonight? I'll chop some wood for you, or help with the chores."

"Sure. There's always wood to be chopped. Nate's over there in the implement shed."

Oscar tied his horse, flung his coat over the seat of the cart, and headed for the shed.

Peter whispered to me tearfully, "He forgot to give me candy." Suddenly he jumped up on the cart, grabbed Oscar's coat, and dug into the pocket, hunting for candy.

"Peter!" I demanded, "stop that and come down!"

"I found some," he giggled happily, pulling out his hand. As he did so, a thick wad of bills fell out and scattered on the lane beside the cart.

I gasped, and quickly stooped to pick them up. They were all $100 bills, and there were a lot of them, at least fifty! I quickly stuffed them all back into the coat pocket and took a pack of chewing tobacco away from Peter. "That's not candy," I informed him. "We must put it back."

I scolded Peter for trying to steal candy, and for a punishment I sent him to his room for a nap. Meanwhile, I was thinking, Fifty $100 bills would be $5,000! There surely was something strange about this. Why would Oscar pretend to be poor, begging for food, and all the while carrying so much money loose in his pocket?

When I told Nate about it, he blew a long, low whistle of amazement. "It sure looks suspicious. Maybe I should ask if I can borrow some money from him, to see what he says."

"Maybe he has Alzheimer's disease and wandered away from his home with his money," I suggested. "Perhaps his family is frantically searching for him."

At the supper table, Oscar talked nonstop, between mouthfuls.

"Yup, I've found what I'm looking for," he shared with feeling. "I'm going to join the Amish church. You folks are the salt of the earth. You'll help a poor old man like me. You won't let me starve, and you'll give me a pile of hay to sleep on, in the barn."

Oscar rambled on and on about how great the Amish are. When he went outside, I got a bucket of hot water and Lysol disinfectant, and washed the chair he sat on, the doorknobs, and whatever else he might have touched. I wasn't taking any chances. 🍂

December 14

I spent the day with Grandma Annie. She had a comforter knotting for the neighborhood women, and as usual, the tongues flew faster than fingers and needles. It was interesting to hear the different theories about Oscar Thompson.

One said she wouldn't be surprised to hear that he's an

escaped prisoner, using this ruse as an Amishman to hide from the police. Another suspected he might be a child molester, and someone wondered if he was a thief, although no one reported anything missing when he was around.

Emanuel Fannie (wife of Emanuel) expressed her opinion that he's eccentric and senile, but harmless. Nate and I had decided to say nothing about his wad of money to others. Sooner or later his intentions will come to light.

Oscar attended church on Sunday, and he stayed for dinner, although somebody reported that he doesn't think much of our simple, common church meals. He likes good cooking, and he was heard to say he needs more than pickles, red beets, smearcase, and *Schnitzboi* (apple pie) to keep him going.

He must've had a kind of Christian teaching some time or other, for he sure can talk religion, and he knows the hymns. Maybe he had a Christian mother who tried to train him and teach him in the Christian life. 🍂

December 22

*T*his afternoon we attended the Christmas program at Dora's school. She had already been talking about it for several weeks, learning her lines and singing Christmas carols. The windows were decorated with paper snowflakes, and the blackboards with lovely freehand winter scenes done in colored chalk. Colorful paper chains hung from wall to wall.

I had to think back to last year when Dora went to public school and they put up a brightly decorated Christmas tree in the gymnasium. Dora begged and begged for us to put up and decorate a tree, too. This year I haven't heard a word about it, I guess because none of her Amish friends have Christmas trees.

The first and second graders sang a song by themselves, their childish, innocent voices blending beautifully. Dora's rose above the rest as they sang.

> O beautiful star of Bethlehem,
>   Shining afar through shadows dim,
> Give us the light to light the way
>   Unto the land of perfect day.
> For Jesus is now that star divine;
>   Brighter and brighter he will shine.
> O beautiful star of Bethlehem,
>   Shine on. . . .
>
> —*Unknown*

After that, the older children had a play, then each recited a poem, and more carols were sung by all. Peter enjoyed it immensely, and I'm glad, for next year he will probably have a part in it. Teacher Ruth gave each of the pupils a small gift.

We all trudged happily home through the falling snow. Once again, I thanked God for the privilege of having our own schools. ❦

YEAR ELEVEN

♥

Joy Overflowing

January 26

*B*rrr! It's cold! 15 degrees below zero this morning! It feels cozy sitting by the stove, feet in the bake oven, with a dish of freshly exploded popcorn and a bowl of juicy red apples beside me. The sun shone brightly this afternoon and warmed things up considerably, and the children begged to go skating.

Dora didn't have much chance yet to try out her new skates, and Peter has a little pair, too, this year. So we bundled up and headed for the "island" as we call it. On one side of it the water stands still, almost like a pond, and there it freezes solid if it gets cold enough. We saw a muskrat house (a neat mound made of mud and grass) and frozen reeds and the lovely winter landscape.

The children had great fun, slipping, sliding, and falling down, laughing and getting up again, then soon flopping down again. As I sat on the bank watching them, thinking that learning to skate is a bit like learning to walk in the Spirit and living the Christian life. So often we fall and have to pick ourselves up, ask for forgiveness, and start over again.

"Wherefore, seeing we are compassed about with so great a cloud of witnesses, let us lay aside every weight and the sin which does so easily beset us." "Let him who thinks he stands, take heed lest he fall." ❧

I took the quilt top I'm embroidering and spent the day with Barbianne. She's flat on her back in bed, and it gets lonely for her, I'm sure. She's been having pregnancy complications, and the doctor ordered complete bed rest. Her thirteen-year-old sister is boarding there and goes to school from there.

When I walked into her room, she exclaimed, "Oh, you can't imagine how glad I am to see you! This gets so boring and lonely lying here."

I thought back to what an outdoor girl Barbianne had been, running out to Rudy whenever she could, hitching up the horses, bouncing out the lane on the wagon, her prayer covering flying straight back in the wind, going for a daring motorcycle ride with a neighbor boy, and helping with chores rather than housework.

Now she is forced to lie still in bed, not knowing how long, or what the outcome will be. This is what we say yes to when we get married, I thought. It may mean giving up our health and strength, complications, life-threatening situations, forced bed rest. Whatever happens, we yield ourselves to God's work in our lives. It's good that we don't know everything beforehand.

A man, when he marries, takes upon himself the burden and responsibility of providing for his wife and children, paying the bills, food, clothing, school expenses, doctor bills, heating, rent or mortgage payments. . . . Those things are on his shoulders, a burden he cannot lay down.

I thought of the saying, "Needles and pins, needles and pins, when you get married, your trouble begins." Yet in my experience, the good far outweighs the bad.

"What's new?" Barbianne asked. "Time seems to crawl while I'm in bed. I've never enjoyed reading, and I can't crochet or embroider while lying down. Sometimes I feel like sneaking out of bed and doing my work, or going outside for fresh air."

" 'In your patience possess your souls,' " I quoted. "I know it's easier for me to say that than for you to wait."

"I agree. But having company helps to pass the time. Let's talk all afternoon."

And so we did, about most anything, from having babies, to the hereafter.

"Sometimes the thought of bringing a new little soul into this wicked world frightens me so much that I think I wouldn't care if I'd lose the baby," Barbianne admitted. "Other times I so desperately want the baby that I'm not above bargaining with God for its survival. I can't understand myself at all."

"I've had such thoughts myself," I confided to her. "What if one of these precious little souls would fall into sin and reap the bitterness that comes from disobedience? Then I remind myself that we have the remedy for sin, Jesus, the redeemer who can wash away every stain of sin and make us completely whole."

"That's what Rudy told me," Barbianne responded. "He says we have a priceless heritage for our children, and it's not like they'd be born to ungodly parents in the slums of a wicked city, or something like that. But still, I feel so inexperienced and inadequate."

"It's good if we feel that way," I reminded her. "Then we rely more on God's help. Being a parent is such a big responsibility, and God is willing to help us with it, if we humbly walk with him day by day."

"I've been praying a lot," she admitted, half shyly. "I want to fortify myself for the task and also for submission if I lose the baby . . . and for patience to endure this bed rest."

She smiled bravely, and I squeezed her hand. I think God is preparing her to be a mother. ❧

April 6

*T*hese past few weeks have been rather grim, and I'm counting the days until our visitor leaves. We've taken our turn in giving old Mandy Miller a home. She's a great-aunt to most of the Millers in this community, and they've taken turns keeping her. But since she's quite a care and becoming too much of a burden, they asked for help from nonrelatives.

I don't know if she has Alzheimer's, is just senile, or has hardening of the arteries. At any rate, she's childish, contrary, and hard to please. I feel so tied down when outside the robins are joyously singing, the wind is warm and scented of flowers and woodland and freshly plowed earth, and the daffodils and hyacinths are blooming. All this is calling for me to come out and enjoy it, but I can't.

Mandy's walking goes poorly, but the minute I go outside, she's up and stirring around in my drawers and throwing things out. This morning when I took her a bowl of oatmeal and milk for breakfast, she protested, "No, I want an egg and scrapple."

So I gave the oatmeal to Nate and made her an egg and scrapple. By that time she had changed her mind, and announced, "No, I want oatmeal."

"The oatmeal is all gone now," I told her. "Eat the egg." She began to cry piteously, and I felt like a tyrant.

On Monday morning I came in from hanging up wash and found that Mandy had put a kettle of water on the stove and put her nightcap in it. "See, I'm making soup," she announced, happily stirring it.

I thought she was still in bed. I have to watch her carefully, for the other day I found her just ready to reach right into a kettle of boiling noodle water. I snatched her hands away, and she complained, "But I wanted to wash my hands."

I think it does us good to see how a person can become, to remind us that the time to serve the Lord and "work out our salvation" is when we still have our sound minds. Just a few years ago she was still all right, an intelligent and discreet woman, and a pillar of faith and good works in the church. If we'd have a choice, likely we'd all choose to die a little sooner rather than to go through something like that.

Mandy has the same name as our angel girl (Amanda), and I keep reminding myself that she is safe in the arms of Jesus and spared such experiences. From now on, I want to be more mindful of those who all the time are caring for an invalid or aged parents. I will do what I can to lighten their load or help them. 🐚

May 13

*P*riscilla and Miriam walked over this afternoon. We sat in the shade of the lavender, heavenly scented lilac bush and had a long talk.

Miriam is now two and a half, and she and Crist are quite a pair for getting into mischief. In the barn they chased the banties, in the garden they pulled big handfuls of onions and radishes much too small for the table, and in the barnyard they fed the horse a between-meal snack, something Nate had strictly forbidden.

Priscilla was willing to talk about their spiritual and church problems today, something she has not often done. "It started when Jack Groff started going with Henry's carpenter crew. Jack used to be a member of a strict plain church, but he left because he wanted a TV set. He was trying to justify himself by watching the plain people and pointing out inconsistencies he thought he saw.

"Henry and Jack became good friends, and Jack and his wife, Glenda, came to our house a lot. Their opinions and prejudices began to rub off on us."

Priscilla sat in deep thought, plucking absentmindedly at a piece of grass, then went on.

"At first we argued about it a lot, and for a while I was defending our way of life. Then believe it or not, later it was the other way around, with me floundering and Henry sticking up for the Amish. Finally, we stopped talking about it altogether.

"The Groffs persuaded us to go with them to their church a few times, but I didn't feel at home there. All this was putting a strain on our marriage. We seemed to have no peace and happiness. Even now yet, there's a rift between us that I wish I'd know how to solve."

Priscilla brushed a few tears out of her eyes. We sat in silence for a few minutes, and I wished I could think of something helpful to say.

Finally Priscilla found her voice again. "The Groffs kept

telling us over and over that there's just as much chance of having pride in plain clothes and plain living, as there is in having the latest styles and luxuries. They were saying, 'Why do you think being plain is better in God's eyes?' and 'Do you think you're going to earn favor in God's sight by doing without something?'

"They were so sure of themselves, so convincing. According to them, we could have the luxuries and modern conveniences of our day and still get to heaven. They pointed out any flaws they could think of, and all this began to wear down our convictions.

"I think we're both thoroughly confused. We still have enough convictions left to keep us from leaving, but not enough to give us peace, happiness, and contentment like we had before."

Priscilla sighed. "I wish we still had peace. Feeling dissatisfied is not a good feeling."

My heart ached for her and Henry. "Have you prayed for God to show his will to you and give you peace?" I asked.

"Yes, we have, but it seems like our prayers bounce off the ceiling."

Just then Henry drove in to pick up Priscilla and Miriam. His horse didn't want to stand, and they had to go right away, I sat there deep in thought after they had gone, wishing I could have helped Priscilla more.

Last fall Henry and Priscilla had put away all that was forbidden in the *Ordnung* (church rules) and had partaken of communion again, but this spring they haven't been attending services. They were still torn by indecision, and I sat there thinking of what I might have said to make things clear to Priscilla.

Sadie came to me with a dainty little bouquet of fragrant

lilies of the valley and sat by me in the grass. A bee buzzed lazily in the sweet-scented lilacs.

"Mam, are there flowers in heaven?" Sadie asked, in that sweet, childish voice of hers. "I wish I could give these lilies of the valley to Amanda."

"I don't think we can know for sure, but we know it's a beautiful place, where no one is ever sad. Jesus wipes away all tears, and there is singing and rejoicing."

I felt a bug crawling on my neck, and I quickly slapped at it, but it had crawled to the other side. I swatted again. Next I felt it on my cheek and I made a grab for it. Then I heard a chuckle behind me, and Nate dropped to the grass beside me, twirling a foxtail weed in his hand.

"Is something bothering you, that you're sitting so still?" he asked. "You're usually on the go from dawn to dusk."

I nodded, waited until Sadie had run off to play, and unburdened my story. "It's Priscilla. She finally told me some of their conflicts." I shared the whole story with him.

"But that's beside the point," Nate responded. "If there's such a great danger in having pride in separation from the world, do the Groffs think we should indulge in questionable things, just to make sure we don't have pride in not doing them?

"In Jesus' story of the publican and the Pharisee, what if the publican had overheard the Pharisee saying, 'I fast twice a week, I give tithes of all I possess, I'm not an adulterer nor an extortioner, and I'm not sinful like other men are,' and thought to himself, Well, that Pharisee is proud! In righteousness there is pride, so I'm going to continue in my sins. Being righteous is just as wrong because then you have pride.

"I think it's high time for the ministers to visit Henry and

Priscilla again, to explain some things a bit better. Apparently the Groffs have influenced them to believe that we deprive ourselves of luxuries and conveniences in order to earn God's favor and salvation. They have the cart before the horse. I think I'll go over to Emanuel Yoder tonight and talk to him about going to see Henry and Priscilla."

I was glad to see that Nate was concerned and willing to do something about it. Maybe soon Henry and Priscilla can see things more clearly again and can find peace in giving up their wills and surrendering all to Christ. ❧

June 13

*W*hat Is Prayer?

A mighty force that flows along
   In silent currents swift and strong;
A love that reaches everywhere
   In gentle blessing—that is prayer.

Unuttered longing that is heard
   Before the sound of spoken word;
Courage to do and strength to dare
   Meekly and humbly—that is prayer.

Desire made holy; hope on wings;
   The calm sweet trust that leaves all things
To wise God's unfailing care:
   This quiet confidence is prayer.
                              —*Bonnie Day*

Prayer, is it really a love that reaches everywhere in gentle blessing? I believe it is. If we pray for others and don't have love for them, our prayers probably are not very effective. Someone else may be able to pray the prayer of faith for them.

In our prayers for Henry and Priscilla, Nate and I have been feeling a calm, sweet trust and a quiet confidence. It's like a burden rolled off our backs and onto the Burden-Bearer. We have given it all into his hands.

I'm feeling stiff and sore tonight from picking so many peas and strawberries. The children are a big help, but it's not like having Barbianne and Rudy to help. Nate helps whenever he can, which is not often. Between milking and haymaking, he's kept rather busy.

Pamela Styer came and helped pick berries this forenoon—she even helped to cap them and ladle the hot jam into jars for canning. She's a good egg, always ready to help in whatever way she can. I've often wondered whether she is a believer, but somehow, I've never had the spunk to ask her. She's so capable and self-confident. If she'd be crying and in need of help like Dottie Rogers was, then it would be easier to broach the subject.

It feels good to relax here on the back porch with a refreshing breeze bringing me the scent of the red rambler roses on the old trellis, happy shouts and laugher of the children as they play under the trees, and the clatter of the horse-drawn mowing machine as Nate mows the hayfield.

The constant pain of having to part with Amanda is gone, the wound is mostly healed, and the sorrow is a memory, like sweet, sad strains of music in the night. I have gone through the valley of the shadow, through doubts, fears, and discouragement, but my faith has emerged victorious, brighter and clearer for having been forged in the fire.

Occasionally I have a fresh pang of grief, but I know that if I walk with Jesus, I will someday have my little angel girl back, that I will be where she is.

"I know Christ Jesus, whom I have believed, and am persuaded that he is able to keep that which I have committed unto him against that day." ❧

June 28

I will mention the lovingkindnesses of the Lord, and the praises of the Lord, according to all that the Lord has bestowed on us."

The children found a bantam hen sitting on a nest of eggs out behind the barn, and every day they were running out to check on her. Today they came dashing in, shouting, *"Die Bieblin briehe aus!* (the chicks hatched)." Such cute little balls of fluff!

The mother hen is very protective and in a moment's time can have those twelve chicks all gathered underneath her wings. I marvel at how promptly obedient those peeps are! I think of Jesus' words: "How often would I have gathered your children together even as a hen gathers her chickens under her wings, but you would not."

Jesus is calling us to him, saying, "Come unto me, all you that labor and are heavy laden, and I will give you rest." Under his wings there is peace, shelter, and safety from the evil one, but so often we want to go our own willful selfish way and wander away from him and into sin and heartache. How sad!

Yesterday we had a rainy day, and in the afternoon Peter came in, holding something behind his back, his brown eyes shining with happiness.

"Something for you," he announced. "Dad and I made it."

He held out a homemade bluebird house, just what I had for long been wishing for. I thanked and hugged him, and he ran off happily, saying they were making three more. We've been hearing and seeing bluebirds around here lately, and we hope if we provide nesting places, they'll decide to stay.

Oh, heavenly Father, thank you for the wondrous blessings you bestow on us every day. Help us pause to appreciate the beauties of nature around us, to marvel at the intricacies of your handiwork. 🐦

July 3

*B*eautiful summer weather. The garden looks nice. We had our first meal of corn on the cob and are anxiously watching for the first ripe tomato. The lima beans are hanging on nicely, and I believe it will be a bumper crop. Nothing beats fresh garden goodies, picked young and tender just a short time before it is served. We feel thankful for the abundant rainfall and for the sunshine which makes things grow.

Henry came over last week with a cute, fat little pony in a trailer. Since a friend of his is looking for a good home for it, he wondered whether we wanted it. Nate started to say that our children are too young for a pony, but Dora and Peter protested so strongly that he relented.

Grandpa Dave said there's an old pony cart in their barn, and he believes it would still be usable if repaired. So all we needed yet was a harness, which we borrowed on Friday, and now the children are happily going for rides whenever they're allowed to.

We named the pony "Merrylegs" after the pony in *Black Beauty*. He is quite tame and too fat to go fast. Even Cristly can drive him. It looks so cute seeing them all piled into the cart, rosy cheeked and happy, and the pony trotting about with them. Are we thankful enough for their exuberant good health, or do we take it for granted? Good health is such a blessing, and I'm afraid too often we don't realize that until it's gone.

Oh, God, thank you for our lovely, healthy children. Help us to train them right, so it will be easy for them to give their hearts to you. Send them guardian angels to keep them safe from danger, harm, and evil, both physical and spiritual. ❧

August 7

Mr. and Mrs. Rogers paid us a much-appreciated visit last evening and had a surprise to show us—a new little son, just four weeks old, healthy, howling, beautiful! They are overjoyed, and I don't blame them a bit. Stacey is now five years old, and sweet and lovable as ever, in spite of being a Down's syndrome child.

They came in a pickup truck, and the back of it was filled with chocolate candy! The children's eyes simply bulged, and I think mine did, too.

Mr. Rogers or a friend of his, I'm not sure which, works

at a candy "factory," and these were rejects, perhaps for a wrong ingredient. So he brought them to us, saying we could feed them to the cows and hogs. That would be all right, but how am I to keep the children out of it? They love the sticky stuff, and already they are beginning to come in for meals with no appetite whatsoever. Sigh!

I've been having visions of them all coming down with appendicitis, diabetes, or whatever it is that too much sweets cause. Maybe I could put a sign at the end of the lane saying FREE CHOCOLATE CANDY and see how soon the carriages start coming in the lane. Or dump it into the creek.

Cristly asked me if I thought the cows would give chocolate milk now. I'm hoping it will at least boost their milk production for a few weeks! 🐛

August 15

*T*he words of a wise man's mouth are gracious." At last our long-dreamed-of trip is becoming a reality. We are making plans to visit Isaac and Rosemary in Minnesota!

My idea of Barbianne and Rudy babysitting for us is out, for she is due to deliver soon now. So we're taking all of our children along.

I'm feeling atwitter, for I've never traveled out of state before, except on our depressing trip to Toronto. Surely this will be a joyous trip instead of a sad one. Sometimes I feel as if I should pinch myself to see if it's for real, or if I'll wake up and it was all a dream.

There are suitcases to pack, clothes to get ready, and a

hundred little details to take care of. Emanuel Yoder's son will do our milking and feed the animals. I'm hoping for a dry spell so the grass won't grow too fast and the weeds in the garden won't take over.

Blessedly my big batch of Silver Queen sweet corn was ready for canning last week, so I won't have to worry about that anymore. The Summer Rambo apples will wait until I get back.

Dora and Peter together are energetically pushing the reel mower over the lawn. Their anticipation gives wings to their feet, and for once they didn't grumble about the job. Sadie and Crist are folding the clean wash, their faces bright, happy, and eager. They're all so tickled to be allowed to go along, I believe they'd be willing to do anything for me.

"Your testimonies have I taken as an heritage for ever, for they are the rejoicing of my heart."

August 17

*A*s we meet and touch each day
The many travelers on our way,
Let every such brief contact be

A glorious helpful ministry;
The contact of the soil and seed,
  Each giving to the other's need,
Each helping on the other's best,
  And blessing each, as well as blest.
  —*Susan Coolidge*

I'm keeping notes while on our train ride en route to Minnesota. So many different kinds of people traveling on this train. A fat, roly-poly man came over to us, wondering about our clothes and our customs. He asked about my bonnet and shawl, and Nate's broad-rimmed hat and plain suit.

"Why do you wear black?" he wanted to know. "Is this a part of your religion?"

He asked one question after the other, and Nate patiently answered each one. When I went to the rest room, a young girl asked me whether I'm a nun! I wish we wouldn't attract attention like this. Yet we will try to answer kindly and sincerely if someone asks about our faith. I guess we can't blame them for being curious.

The children love traveling on a train, and they try not to miss anything. I hope they're old enough to remember this all their life. At least they didn't have to wait as long for their first train ride as I did.

The motion of the train is making me sleepy, but I have a secret fear that one of the children will be kidnapped if I doze off. It's a foolish fear, on a train, I know.

Oh, God, keep your protecting hand over us all, among these strangers and so far away from home. 🐝

*W*hat a blessing it was to step into Rosemary's cheery, homey kitchen. It was like a bit of heaven to me, to be welcomed so warmly, and ushered in like that, after being among strangers and traveling so far. Rosemary was smiling and gracious as always, and the children (ours and theirs) hit it off together right away and ran off to play. I hoped they wouldn't fall into any hay holes, manure pits, or wells.

Nate helped Isaac repair fences since his cows were out last night. Rosemary and I had the kitchen to ourselves to have a good, old-fashioned chat once again, yes, to talk to our heart's content! She really does like it here in Minnesota, and they are busy and happy. They haven't made much financial headway yet but have had plenty to eat and clothes to wear.

"We're poor farmers," she admits, "but God has blessed us abundantly in many ways, and we are rich in love. What more could one ask for?" It's true—the best things in life are things that money can't buy.

She showed me her yard and garden. Things are a bit later here than at home, but they had more rainfall, longer summer days, and everything's still green. They live in a beautiful valley with nice scenery all around, and I'm sure I could make myself at home here.

The Amish families built a little one-room schoolhouse, where Matthew is already in fourth grade. Perhaps the next time I see him, he'll already be *rumschpringing* (running around with the youth).

I helped Rosemary pick and *blick* (hull) lima beans for supper, and we dug new potatoes. She had a rooster roasting in the oven in the washhouse, to keep the kitchen cool. Isaac brought in golden ears of sweet corn and big vine-ripened tomatoes. The home-cooked meal smelled so good after train fare and sandwiches.

As we all sat around the big table in the kitchen, enjoying Rosemary's country cooking, talking, and reminiscing, I looked at each face around the table. My heart overflowed with gratitude and love.

I thought back to one evening when Isaac was still a widower and I was working for him. Nate had come to pick me up in his trottin' buggy with his sorrel horse, and Isaac had gone to woo Rosemary, and now—all these little faces around the table. There was only one ache in my heart—the little missing face, Amanda's. ❦

August 20

When we arrived in Minnesota, one of the first questions from Isaac and Rosemary was about how Henry and Priscilla are relating to the church. We didn't have a favorable report. Isaac was concerned, and he said he's going to write to them. He and Henry had been good friends while Henry boarded with them, and they had regarded each other with mutual respect.

"I guess he must not yet have been rooted and grounded in the faith as strongly as we thought," Isaac remarked thoughtfully, his face lined with sadness. "Maybe he wasn't aware of the pitfalls and dangerous influences around us. It's too bad his co-worker was a hindrance to him. Maybe he would've been better off farming, as he thought at first he'd like to do."

"Perhaps Priscilla wasn't the helpmeet she could have been," Rosemary suggested. "Maybe she was weak in the faith, too."

"They don't talk much about it," I told her. "We have the same questions that you do and are left wondering if there is anything we can do to help them."

"Why don't we kneel and have a silent prayer for Henry and Priscilla," Isaac proposed. "This is a heavy burden on my heart."

I felt a mixture of awe and respect for Isaac. He was taking his ministerial calling seriously and had a heartfelt concern for the sheep of the flock, to keep them safely in the fold, even though they weren't a member of his district.

After breakfast Isaac hitched two horses to the market wagon, and we all piled in. They took us around visiting other Amish families in the area. It was an interesting and worthwhile day.

One family has a ten-year-old child completely blind and helpless since birth, and a man who suffered a stroke three years ago and since then is in bed, completely helpless. When we see such circumstances, it reminds us to thank God each day for good health.

We had to leave for the bus station at 4:30 p.m. On the way home, we planned to spend a few days visiting in Holmes County, Ohio. Rosemary prepared an early supper, and soon afterward, Isaac hitched a fresh horse to the spring wagon to take us to the station. After our tearful good-byes had been said, we started off, waving to Rosemary and the children until we rounded a corner and could no longer see them.

We had gone only a few miles when the left front wheel hit a pothole. The spring wagon lurched to the side and tilted precariously. Before I thought of what I was doing, I screamed, although now I'm ashamed of doing so. I grabbed for Sadie and Crist. We all jumped off and in a moment saw that the wheel had broken off.

"Ei-yi-yi!" Isaac exclaimed in disbelief, and I grinned at the expression on his face. "That has never happened to me before." He shook his head.

"Maybe you never before had such a load along." Nate chuckled as he consoled Isaac.

The children laughed hilariously, but I couldn't see much humor in the situation. I was afraid we'd be late at the station and miss the bus.

But then, a kindly looking elderly man, driving past in a car, saw our dilemma, stopped, and wondered if we needed help. Isaac asked if he would please kindly drive us to the bus station.

He said he'd be glad to, and we made it on time. I believe God sent him there just when we needed him. There would be lots more to write, but I'm so sleepy that my eyes keep falling shut and my writing sounds stilted and unnatural. ❧

August 27

*E*ast, west, home's best! Home again, and it was true—"be it ever so humble, there's no place like home" (Payne). Henry and Priscilla were here. They had mowed the lawn and were busily weeding the garden, as a surprise for us! We caught them in the act, and I felt a rush of gratitude toward them for being so kind and helpful.

They stayed for supper, prepared by Priscilla, and Henry helped with the chores. When Grandpa Daves came after supper, we sat on the porch, talked about our trip, and caught up on local news of things that happened while we were gone.

It was a lovely, twilight evening. Frogs were croaking their poignant evening song, down by the creek. Our children joined Miriam in chasing fireflies, and their laughter floated up to us, mingled with the chorus of the katydids and other night insects. A few stars twinkled in the dusky sky, and my heart was flooded with mysterious contentment and joy. It was so good to be home again, among these dear, familiar sounds and surroundings. God "has has made everything beautiful in its time."

"Did you hear about Oscar Thompson?" Grandpa Dave asked, breaking into my reverie. "They say he's been picked up by the police ten miles east of here. He was arrested and jailed for robbing a bank in Tennessee! A crook, that's what he was! And here we thought he was a harmless half-wit, pretending to be an Amishman. . . .

"Ha! You never know about these outsiders. . . . It sure is necessary to make them prove—" Suddenly he stopped short, thinking about Henry. Henry had been an outsider, and now. . . .

Priscilla got up, saying it was Miriam's bedtime and they should be leaving. The atmosphere seemed strained as they said their good-byes and left. My heart ached for them both, and I wanted to call out to them, Come back! You are one of us. Don't leave! Don't force us to shun you and put you in the ban. We want you and need you! You don't need to be outsiders.

The joy and peace of the evening had vanished, and

sadness descended on us, like the heavy dew settling on the grass. ❧

August 30

*Y*esterday morning I woke to the familiar sound of the banty rooster crowing his welcome to the new day. I was thinking, How nice to wake up in my own bed.

I was singing as I sliced the mush into the pan to fry it and put on a kettle of water for the oatmeal with raisins. When I ran to the milk house for a pitcher of milk, a carriage was coming in the lane, and it was Grandpa Dave.

"Good morning!" I called cheerily. "You're up bright and early."

Suddenly I noticed that Dave was neither smiling nor talking—a sure sign that something was wrong.

"Did you hear about Rudys?" he asked.

I shook my head numbly. Was he once again the bearer of bad news?

"Barbianne's in the hospital. They had a stillborn son last night. They will just have graveside services, and the burial will be this afternoon around 2:00."

He turned the horse around to leave, without another word.

My heart contracted with pain, and tears pushed at my eyelids. Oh, God, why?

I remembered the conversation I had with Barbianne months ago. The baby would've been loved and welcomed by kind and caring parents. On him would have descended a wonderful Christian heritage. What must it be

152

like joyously to await the birth of a baby, who then arrives not healthy, squirming, and lustily crying, but still, with the pall of death over it?

Barbianne came home from the hospital this forenoon, and this afternoon I walked over to see her. She sat on the rocker, her face pale with its baptism of pain, and her eyes dark with sorrow.

"Dave Annie [Dave's wife, Annie] was just here, and she said something that hurt me horribly," Barbianne moaned in anguish. "She said the baby is better off this way. Why would my baby be better off dead? Why would anyone be born at all, if they're better off dead?

"If our boy had lived, he could have helped others, worked to make this a better world, and loved and encouraged others."

Her words came in torrents until she broke off in tears. I cried with her, wishing I would know how to comfort her. Just being there and listening seemed to mean something to her.

Finally I was able to piece a few words together. "Someday we'll understand the whys and wherefores of undeserved pain, and God's plan will be made known to us. But for now, we only 'see through a glass, darkly.' We only see the hanging threads, the ragged underside of the pattern God is weaving in our lives. We'll have to trust that all things work together for good to those who love God, and that God makes no mistakes."

Barbianne nodded meekly. "I will try to accept it and to trust like you said. But I never dreamed it would be so hard to give up my baby. Maybe when the ache in my heart grows a little less, I'll be able to accept it better."

As I walked home through the fields, I thought that Barbianne and Rudy might be finding it harder to accept their loss because this was their first baby and they have no other children. However, I still think that if they'd have had him to love for a few years and then had to give him up, it might have been harder still—as with our Amanda.

Yet who can measure grief? No matter how deep the hurt, God will bind up our wounds and heal our broken hearts, if we surrender everything to him and trust him. ℰ

September 3

*A*lready it's like fall, the days are crisp and cool, and silo filling has started. I'm hoping we won't have an early frost, for it would spite me for my garden things. Likely we'll have a heat wave before autumn comes to stay.

Today was the first day of school for Dora and Peter, and they were both eager to go. Peter put on his new strawhat and proudly carried his lunch bucket. How nice that they don't have to go into town on a school bus and that they have an Amish teacher.

Last week we mothers got together and cleaned the schoolhouse, sweeping down cobwebs, scrubbing desks, blackboards, walls, floors, and windows. Now it's sparkling clean for the first day of school.

This year the parents plan to take turns bringing hot noon meals to school one day a week, so the children have a change from the usual packed lunch. Then we'll stay and visit the rest of the afternoon, showing our interest and how important school is.

This is quite different from the parent-teacher meetings

they had in public school. Dora won't have to be ashamed of us now—we'll be dressed exactly like the other parents.

At the supper table Nate asked Peter, "Well, what did you learn at school today?"

"I learned how to snap paper wads with my suspenders."

I suppose Teacher Ruth will have her hands full with him. ❧

October 7

*O*n the maple trees,
  the scarlet leaves hang shining in the breeze;
And the brown stubble fields are crisp and sere,
  Touched by the hoarfrost of the waning year.
  —*Unknown*

Fire in the range feels good this morning. I'm drying a pan of yellow Delicious apples on top of the stove, and it's filling the kitchen with a delightful, sweet, tangy aroma.

The merits of the old kitchen range are varied and many, and I wonder why some folks prefer gas or oil heat. Besides cooking and baking with it and drying *Schnitz* (sliced apples) on top, the range heats water in the reservoir and teakettle for a variety of purposes—doing dishes, washing laundry, and taking baths.

Clothing can be dried around its glowing warmth (who needs an electric clothes dryer) and sadirons heated for ironing clothes.

What feels better on a cold winter evening when you come in, half frozen from doing outdoor chores, than to stick your feet into the bake oven until they're toasty warm? The pipe shelf is great for drying mittens, and the warming closet keeps crackers and pretzels from getting stale.

The children like to make potato chips by laying thin sliced potatoes on top of the stove until they're golden brown on each side, then sprinkling them with salt.

Last but not least is its usefulness in making toast. We either place bread slices on back of the stove for a while or spear the bread with a fork, lift the lid, and toast it over the flame. Such toast is easy to make, economical, and delicious.

To my way of thinking, chopping wood and carrying coal and ashes is well worth all these benefits. What would a farmhouse be without the good old cookstove? When the electric goes off during a storm, we're snug and warm, while our *englisch* neighbors are without heat.

When Nate and Peter came in from doing the chores, Peter sniffed the air, and said, "Dried apple *Schnitz!* I want to take some in my lunch today."

He and Dora both are still enchanted with going to school, and I sure hope it lasts. We would find it hard to force them to go against their wishes. ❧

October 8

*T*oday I cleaned out the washhouse attic. There was an accumulation of old stuff from years ago. Some of it I decided to throw out, but in the drawer of an old nightstand, I found a motto with the following on it:

A Happy Home Recipe

4 cups love
2 cups loyalty
3 cups forgiveness
1 cup friendship
1 large bunch smiles
5 spoons hope

2 spoons tenderness
4 quarts faith
1 barrel laughter
3 pints of
   consideration
   for others

Take love and loyalty, mix thoroughly with faith.
Blend with togetherness, kindness, understanding.
Add hope, friendship, abundant laughter.
Top freely with smiles and consideration for others.
Bake with bright sunshine.
Serve daily in generous helpings.

—Bradley Tyler

I thought long thoughts about when Nate's dad and mom were master and mistress of this house. Nate was a sturdy little chap like Peter, with older brothers and sisters. They were a happy family here, with abundant laughter, loyalty, togetherness, love, forgiveness, and tenderness, all topped with smiles and baked in sunshine, as the verse says.

I resolved to try to serve this recipe in generous helpings to my family. I hope that when I am old and the children are grown, they will have only happy memories of their childhood home and remember me as kind and understanding, not bossy and snappy.

Oh God, help me to keep that resolution the best I can, and when I fail, to remember that the mercies of the Lord are new every morning, that each day is a fresh beginning, a new opportunity to do better. 🌿

*T*his morning I had just filled the washing machine with hot water to do the laundry, when Nate came into the washhouse. I was about to say, "Good, now you can start the engine," when I saw the look on his face.

"What's wrong?" I asked, alarmed. His face was positively gray, ashen and drawn.

"Pamela Styer just stopped in a minute ago," he said gravely. She had Grandpa Daves along and was on her way to pick up Priscilla to take her to the hospital. Henry was in an accident, and he's badly hurt."

"What happened?" I asked dumbly, leaning against the washtub for support. "Will he live?"

Nate shrugged his shoulders. "He was hit by a truck and was unconscious. I guess time will tell. I'll finish the chores now."

I watched as Nate walked to the barn, shoulders slumped forward like an old man.

A few minutes later Pamela's car was in the drive again, and Priscilla brought Miriam in. There was a haunted look on her face. She left without a word.

The morning seemed to drag, and it was all I could do to get the wash on the line. I felt weak and drained. Sadie, Crist, and Miriam played happily together with the Lego building blocks.

At 10:00 o'clock Gloria Graham stopped in and said that Priscilla had called and asked her to bring us in to the hospital. I quickly changed my dress, got my shawl and bonnet, and we were soon on our way. We stopped at Emanuel Yoders, and Nate took the children in. What would we do without good neighbors, ready to babysit at a moment's notice?

The ride to the hospital ended all too soon. As we walked through the maze of elevators and hallways, memories came flooding back—most vividly Amanda's hospital stay and my appendectomy, then Priscilla's illness, Nate's food poisoning, and my broken leg years ago. I felt thankful for such a place and for skilled doctors and nurses. Would they be able to help Henry?

Priscilla greeted us outside the intensive-care lobby and motioned for us to follow her. I shuddered as I noticed her eyes—dry, but with pools of grief. I wished I could do something, anything, to erase that haunted look and to make everything all right again for her.

"How is Henry?" Nate searched her face for a clue, but it was expressionless.

"He's not responding," she stated simply.

In a moment we saw the words INTENSIVE CARE blazing in red lights above wide double doors. We went through them, not knowing what to expect. I tried to prepare myself for the worst, but when I saw Henry, I realized I wasn't ready for the shock.

So many wires, tubes and bandages, cables and monitors attached to his head and chest! Since he wasn't breathing on his own, the heart-lung machine caused his chest to rise and fall, filling the room with the sound of artificial breathing. There was a computer screen nearby with a moving red line, likely tracing his heartbeat.

I shuddered, feeling sure that Henry was already dead, that these instruments were just prolonging the agony. I wanted to shout, STOP! Turn off all the machines. This isn't natural. Why don't you let him die in peace?

However, there was nothing to do but return to the waiting room and sit down. Pamela Styer had taken Grandpa Daves home, and we were alone with Priscilla.

"I am the one who is to blame," Priscilla groaned in a tortured voice, choking back a sob. "I encouraged Henry to listen to Jack Groff. I see it all so plainly now. Oh, if only God will let Henry live, I'll be a better wife. . . . I'll be willing to deny self. . . . I'm sure this is a chastening from God."

She was crying in earnest now, her shoulders shaking with convulsive sobs.

I looked helplessly at Nate. What possibly could we say or do to comfort her?

"Let her cry," Nate whispered. "It might be better than to bottle up everything inside."

I gave her a caring hug, and eventually Priscilla's sobs subsided as she fumbled for her handkerchief. "I'm sorry," she said, blowing her nose. "I wasn't planning to act this way."

We talked then, since Priscilla wanted and needed to talk about their problems, hers and Henry's, and difficulties in staying within the *Ordnung* (order) of the church. How shallow their reasoning seemed now in the light of this tragedy. Over and over Priscilla kept saying, "If only God will give us another chance."

We went in to see Henry often, but each time there was no change. At four o'clock Emanuel Yoder came in, and we went home with the driver who had brought him to the hospital. But it seemed as though our hearts stayed in the intensive care unit. Will Henry soon begin to respond? Or—I can't bear to think of the alternative.

Oh God, have mercy . . . and help us to give up our wills

to your perfect will. Help us to do like Emanuel said to us, "*Sei geduldich in allerlei Trübsal* (be patient in every trial)." ❧

*F*aschtdaag (fast day). Once more we spent the greater part of the day fasting and praying for Henry and Priscilla. We did go visiting for awhile this afternoon—over to see Barbianne and Rudy. Their troubles seem small now, compared to yesterday's tragedy.

Grandpa Daves spent the day at the hospital with Priscilla, and tonight we received word that Henry is better, regaining consciousness, and breathing on his own. It sounded much more encouraging. When I heard it, a heavy burden seemed to roll off my back. For the first time since the accident, we have hope that he will recover.

Little Miriam has been with us since yesterday. The house is filled with the sound of the children's laughter and playing. She talks both Dutch and English, and Sadie is picking up English words from her.

We told Miriam about her dad's accident, but I don't think she understands. She went right on playing with her doll and talking to it, as if nothing had happened.

She and Crist are still quite a team for mischief. Tonight while I was out helping with the chores, they sneaked into the pantry and took down the cookie jar. They laid all the cookies out on the shelf and took a bite out of each one. I wonder which one of them thought up that bit of mischief.

This morning in the barn, Dora, Sadie, and Miriam each

got a kitten, put doll dresses and caps on them, wrapped them in dolly quilts, and were playing church. I guess they wanted dolls with faces. Peter was the preacher, and Crist the song leader.

As Peter stood on the barn floor to preach, I heard him say, "There was a man who could not walk, so the people took off part of the roof and lowered his bed into the house where Jesus was, and Jesus made him well. So let's ask Jesus to make Henry well, too."

They all knelt (the kittens, too) around the bales of hay, with bowed heads. I'm trying to impress the scene into my mind, to file it away into my storehouse of precious memories. 🐾

We visited Henry at the hospital tonight and found him dopey but fully conscious. He's still in constant care. He has a long road to recovery, but the outlook is so much brighter than it was. To think that I would have wanted them to turn off the life-support systems! I guess the doctors know what they're doing.

Henry's eyes brightened when we walked in, and Nate clasped his hand. "Pray for me," he muttered weakly. "And . . . I'm sorry."

"Sorry for what?" Nate asked.

Henry closed his eyes for a moment, then said slowly and haltingly, "For not being a faithful church member. I see things differently now . . . much differently. Life is too short. . . . I had my priorities all wrong. If God lets me live, . . . things will be different from now on."

"I'm glad," Nate affirmed him warmly. "Maybe God can make a blessing out of your accident."

"I believe it was a chastening from God," Henry's voice lowered to a whisper. "Pray for me."

Nate assured him that many people were praying for him, and that a lot of prayers were rising to the throne of grace on his behalf.

We didn't stay long, fearing it would tire him. As we left, I felt lighthearted and glad. I believe that everything will work out all right for Henry and Priscilla. "God moves in a mysterious way / His wonders to perform" (Cowper).

"Now no chastening for the present seems to be joyous, but grievous: nevertheless afterward it yields the peaceable fruits of righteousness to those who are exercised thereby." ❧

*T*hanksgiving Day.

"A joyous heart does good like a medicine." We and Grandpa Daves spent the day with Henry and Priscilla and had a time of thanksgiving and rejoicing equal to that of the Pilgrims, in my opinion.

Henry is up and about again, almost back to his usual self, except for his attitude. Now there seems to be a depth of humility, love, and gratitude in him that hadn't been there before, and Priscilla seems radiantly happy again.

Grandma Annie made the pumpkin pies and cake roll, and I furnished the roast turkey with stuffing and gravy.

Henry sat at the head of the table. After we had bowed our heads for a silent prayer of thanksgiving, he cleared his throat and said, "Words cannot begin to express the depth of my gratitude and thankfulness toward God for sparing my life, and toward you folks for all you've done for me. I'm afraid I can never fully repay you. But I believe that someday you'll receive your reward in heaven.

"Priscilla and I have rededicated our lives to God. We intend to serve him with all our hearts, as Titus says, 'denying ungodliness and worldly lusts, to live soberly, righteously, and godly in this present world.' Sometimes when we wander away from God, he has to use drastic events to bring us back to him."

Henry paused to brush away a tear, and Priscilla said, "That's right. God seemed far away, but God wasn't the one who had moved. When we were seeking to serve ourselves, it was impossible for us to stay close to God and to be at peace."

"Praise God!" Grandma Annie exclaimed feelingly.

"This is what we were praying for."

God answered in his own good time, I thought.

Around the table I could see the faces of all my loved ones. Once again my heart filled with gratitude and joy. Our hearts were bound together in love, and hand-in-hand we would journey heavenward. Though oftentimes beset with trials and temptations, our hearts would be filled with joy, for Christ would walk with us, and in his presence is fullness of joy. ❧

December 1

Winter-like winds are howling around the house, and it feels cozy inside baking sugar cookies topped with English walnuts. Pamela Styer just stopped in to bring a phone message. When she saw the cookies, she exclaimed, "Mmmm! I'd like to sink my teeth into one of those."

She did just that and couldn't get done raving over them, how they taste just like the ones Mom used to make. I tossed a dozen into a bag for her—she's done so much for us that we can never repay her.

Between mouthfuls she asked, "How would you like to be a host family for a seventeen-year-old German girl next year?"

"A what?"

Pamela explained what a host family is, that the German girl would live with us and go to school from here. She prefers an Amish family, and that's why Pamela asked us.

I'll have to discuss that with Nate when he comes in. I think it would be interesting sharing our home with a girl from another country, especially a German. I wonder if she would understand the high German we use in church, or maybe even some of our Pennsylvania Dutch.

Yesterday Priscilla and Miriam stopped in for a few minutes on the way to the store. It's so nice to see Priscilla cheerful and happy again, and she and Miriam dressed in humility and according to the *Ordnung* (order). They don't use the electricity in their house anymore and are no longer crowding the fence like they were.

We talked about it, and when Priscilla was ready to leave, she confided to me, "It feels so good to be happy and contented once more. It sure is no fun feeling dissatisfied."

"I'm so glad!" I told her, with deep feeling in my voice. "God does answer prayer, doesn't he?

"Yes! And Henry feels the same way," Priscilla went on, her eyes shining. "His irritability and dissatisfaction are gone, and in its place are peace, happiness, contentment. Our marriage is a hundred percent better. You were right. God gives us peace and happiness when we're willing to give up our own selfish wills."

I watched as she walked to the buggy, leading the skipping Miriam by the hand, and thanked God for his peace that passes all understanding. Truly he does all things well. ❧

December 15

*J*ust a few more pages, and then this journal, too, is completed. At the end of my last journal, I remember, I was wondering whether Nate would have to go to jail, whether we'd have to move into a shack in the woods.

My heart overflows with joy and gratitude that we were spared those hardships. I wouldn't have minded the woods part, though, but I'm glad we can stay here in our charming, old-fashioned farm home by the creek, with the wind mill beside it.

It's a good place for our growing family, away from the temptations and allurements in town. Here, hopefully, we can raise them in the nurture and admonition of the Lord.

Sometimes I wonder what the future holds for each of the children, as they travel the pathways of their lives. Will they have trials and heartaches mixed with the joys, gladness, and sweetness of life? Will they learn to cast all their cares on Jesus, the Burden-Bearer, and trust in him as their Savior and Redeemer?

This is my fervent prayer, for if they have Jesus, they will have everything. If not, though they be rich with this world's goods, they'll have nothing.

May we all live so that we can look forward to that blessed hope of all being together in heaven someday, where there shall be no pain nor crying, and all heartaches and tears shall be wiped away, and joy unspeakable reigns. "At your right hand are pleasures for evermore." ❧

♥ ♥ ♥ ♥ ♥ ♥ ♥ ♥ ♥ ♥ ♥

Scripture References

YEAR EIGHT
Feb. 13: Ps. 103; 1 Sam. 2:1.
June 16: Prov. 14:21.
July 19: Col. 1:12.
Sept. 17: Mark 4:18-19; Matt. 18:10.
Dec. 25: Rom. 8:28.

YEAR NINE
Jan. 30: Isa. 25:8.
Jan. 31: Acts. 20:35; 2 Cor. 9:7.
Feb. 3: Prov. 3:6; Ps. 51:7, 10-12; Ps. 16:11.
Feb. 24: 1 Tim. 6:17.
May 10: Ps. 19:1.
Aug. 17: Prov. 14:12.
Sept. 6: Titus 2:14.
Oct. 11: Phil. 4:8.
Oct. 27: Prov. 22:6.
Nov. 6: Prov. 28:13.
Nov. 10: Matt. 7:12; 25:40.
Nov. 23: Ps. 23:3.
Nov. 24: Rom. 12:10; Eph. 5:22-32.
Dec. 25: Matt. 2; Luke 2.

YEAR TEN
Aug. 29: Matt. 18:10.
Sept. 5: Ps. 34:8.
Oct. 8: Rev. 21—22; James 5:17.
Nov. 9: Matt. 5:13.

YEAR ELEVEN
Jan. 26: Heb. 12:1; 1 Cor. 10:12.
Mar. 3: Luke 21:19.
Apr. 6: Phil. 2:12.
May 13: Luke 18:9-14.
June 13: Ps. 23:4; 2 Tim. 1:12.
June 28: Isa. 63:7; Matt. 23:37; 11:28.
Aug. 15: Eccles. 10:12; Ps. 119:111.
Aug. 20: Gen. 2:18.
Aug. 27: Eccles. 3:11.
Aug. 30: 1 Cor. 13:12; Rom. 8:28.
Oct. 10: Rom. 12:12.
Oct. 11: Mark 2:1-12.
Oct. 12: Heb. 4:16; 12:11.
Nov. 21: Prov. 17:22; Titus 2:12.
Dec. 1: Phil. 4:7; Mark 7:37.
Dec. 15: Ps. 16:11.